WHAT CAN'T

BE UNDONE

WHAT CAN'T
BE UNDONE

Enjoy the ride!

dee

Calgary, June/15

dee
HOBSBAWN-SMITH

thistledown press

Thistledown Press Ltd.
410 2nd Avenue North
Saskatoon, Saskatchewan, S7K 2C3
www.thistledownpress.com

Library and Archives Canada Cataloguing in Publication

Hobsbawn-Smith, Dee, author
What can't be undone / dee Hobsbawn-Smith.

Short stories.
Issued in print and electronic formats.
ISBN 978-1-927068-89-2 (pbk.).–ISBN 978-1-77187-064-1 (html).–
ISBN 978-1-77187-065-8 (pdf)
I. Title.
PS8615.O23W53 2015   C813'.6   C2015-900497-7
C2015-900498-5

Cover and book design by Jackie Forrie
Printed and bound in Canada

Canada Council for the Arts   Conseil des Arts du Canada   SASKATCHEWAN ARTS BOARD   Canadian Heritage   Patrimoine canadien

Thistledown Press gratefully acknowledges the financial assistance of the Canada Council for the Arts, the Saskatchewan Arts Board, and the Government of Canada through the Canada Book Fund for its publishing program.

WHAT CAN'T BE UNDONE

Contents

9   Monroe's Mandolin

21   Nerve

36   The Good Husband

47   Still Life with Birds

61   The Quinzhee

73   Appetites

85   The Pickup Man

99   Other Mothers' Sons

108 Needful Things

123 Fallen Sparrow

145 Exercise Girls

164 Undercurrents

182 The Bridge

Monroe's Mandolin

THE BAR IS JAMMED, PATIENT PEOPLE waiting for the first set. I'm drinking coffee at the counter, my face turned to the stage. Conversation flows around me. Mostly, I don't notice. Tonight, a word dropped into a discussion somewhere behind me hooks my attention.

"It's a Gibson. Want it? Seven hundred."

"Hell, it's a sweet mandolin. Not a mark on her. But I'm not — "

I turn my head in time to see a scrawny redhead four tables back shake his head at a pockmarked man in frayed leather. A small black case lies open on the table in front of them.

" — left-handed, and I don't want the hassle of restringing it. Sorry, man."

In half a heartbeat, I am at the table. "Hey."

"Hey yourself, dollface." Rusty nudges him in the ribs and whispers. Pockface doesn't miss a beat. "Ah. You're Lise, right? You own this joint?" He raises an eyebrow but doesn't protest when I pick up the mandolin.

I nod. "And I'd know this mandolin anywhere. Where'd you get it?"

Pockface's lips purse. He looks at me speculatively. "Sharky's. Pawn shop over on the north side."

"When?"

"Last week. What's it to you?"

"You want to sell it tonight or not?"

Pockface scuffs his boots. "Sure thing. How 'bout seven fifty?"

"Six. Wait here."

Pockface's grimace reveals teeth as ruined as his skin. Rusty shrugs and slips past me, his face averted. Jon, at my elbow within seconds of my signal toward the midlands of the counter, bends close to hear me. "Pay this guy, will you, Jon? Six hundred, and make him sign a receipt. Then tell him to get the hell out. Damn vulture." I lay the mandolin to rest in its case, stare down Pockface, barely raise my voice. "My manager will pay you." The case bumps against my jeans as I head for my office to stash it.

Invoices from the past week are heaped on my desk, awaiting cheques, but I can't settle into a working groove. The mandolin's appearance has short-circuited my routine. I haven't seen Cory for six months. I just bought back his mandolin. Maybe he's alive out there somewhere, I have no way of knowing. That last view of him as we left the walk-in clinic, he wasn't at his best. Not like he is in the photo buried under these damn papers, the man with the golden Gibson, playing at The Foundry's opening. The man he should be. He should be here, I say to myself every morning when I walk into this bar, but saying it doesn't change anything.

Pockface is nowhere in sight when I close my office door on the Gibson. From the hallway that leads to the bar, I hear the band tuning, guitars and piano, the blur of harmonica. The ache in my chest sharpens when I spot Rusty's reflection in the long mirror that lines the hall. He's got an unopened bottle of Johnnie

Walker jammed under his arm and looks surreptitiously around him before he stashes it behind his amp. I just watch. He's got nowhere to run. His eyes, when they meet mine in the mirror, are blue sparks like icebergs colliding. A flush travels up his throat and across his cheeks, and he ducks his head, plugs in his guitar. Halfway into the first verse, the lead singer stops mid-breath.

"Hey, Nathan. You on?"

Rusty kicks his amp. His cheeks are still red. "Dammit. Sorry, Bart."

"Try it again, man."

Jon's bulky shoulders fill the doorway. He's been a bouncer, knows how to occupy space. "I turfed the punk."

"Good. Don't let him back in. You know this guy?" Onstage, Rusty is on his knees, unsnarling wires. "A friend of yours? He boosted a bottle."

"Christ. Not again. That's my little brother Nathan. He just joined the band."

"Ah." Brothers. Tangled.

"I'll make it right."

"Listen, he steals anything else, he's gone." I've run out of charity.

"No drugs, Lise. I swear, he's clean." He smoothes his hand from forehead to nape, his brush cut bristling. "Don't worry about it, I got it covered."

The band spins into the bleak opening bars of Cory's favourite tune, "Barroom Girls." I grab an unused guitar stand and retreat down the hall to my office, but the melody leaks under the door. I collapse in the chair, my throat closing. Jesus. A quick puff on the inhaler. Just a single hit so I can breathe without sounding like a racehorse.

The mandolin's strings quiver under my hands as I take it from its coffin-like case, remembering the day our mother brought it home from a tour through Tennessee. It set her back plenty. The shopkeeper said it had belonged to Bill Monroe, had a faded photo to prove it — the great man in his prime, smiling into the camera, his hands cradling an amber-coloured Gibson. Mom had the thing restrung for her southpaw hands and she played it for years. It sounds undamaged by its travels, and when I run my fingers down the strings, their vibration amplifies the tunes trapped in my throat like asthma. I can't make music and I have more employees than friends. My voice rattles off the walls and windows of my condo, and the odd time I sing here, after hours. But it all comes out flat. I used to say that my business takes all my creative energy, and I blame my asthma for not singing or playing, but that's a lie, even thinner than an E-string. A martyr, Crista calls me. A blocked conduit, I say.

The mandolin is silent as I set it on the stand, run my fingers across its tawny surface. Catch my reflection as I concentrate on locking the door. It could be Crista staring back at me, the same rigid jaw, eyes hemmed by wrinkles. Crista's face is a grid of roads and county lines, her voice a rasp that makes me think of the barbed wire surrounding her ranch. She had entrusted the ranch to the hired man when Mom was diagnosed, sat with us at the hospital for six horrific months, slept with us at the condo every night, cried with us when Mom stopped breathing, took us to the ranch to live. She still calls me every week.

Onstage, the band's first set is wrapping up. Jon catches my eye from his customary spot at the corner of the bar. I work my way around the perimeter. The room is full, tables elbow-tight, crowded with glasses, silent faces turned toward the stage where Rusty is swaying. The spotlights glimmer on his hair, and not for the first time, I wonder, how does it feel to be under those lights, falling into the melody? To be filled by it so completely that it spills out and fills the room too?

Rusty, rapt, is a pale stand-in for my brother. His gnawed fingers build competent chords and runs of melody compared to Cory's dazzle. Bart, at the piano, nods once, Ali slides her voice down the scale, the piano fades. Applause scatter-shots across the room. I bite my tongue when Jon leans in close to make himself heard, his breath on my ear.

"I caught up with Nathan backstage before they started the set. Says it won't happen again . . . You see Cory lately?" When I shake my head, he clucks like a broody hen and marches to the rear of the room. Rusty hops off the stage behind him.

"Hey. Rusty." Rusty swivels and comes back, stops in front of me. "You want to keep playing in my bar? You get no more chances. Hear me?" He shunts out the back door without meeting my eyes.

That was gratuitous, Jon has it handled. But Rusty's here and Cory's not.

When I see Cory next, he'll have a new tune. He always does. I'm glad to hear him play, but I cut him off whenever he tries to tell me anything about that other world that owns him. The eyes of the musicians I hire reflect me as signer of cheques and booker of gigs. No more and no less. My inheritance — our mother's music catalogue — I parlayed into a down payment on The Foundry five years ago. I told myself it would give Cory a refuge if he ever reclaims himself. That it had nothing to do with me, or with what I want. But my life is locked into these bricks and boards. Cory's has gone to waste. I don't know anymore if I am looking for hope in my twin's life or in my own.

I track down Sharky's in the morning.

"We put that mandolin out last winter, took forever to move it," says the bored clerk in her metal cage.

"How much did you give the guy who brought it in?"

"Ya really need to know?"

"It was my mother's mandolin. I'm trying to track down my brother. Please." She studies my face for a minute. It occurs to me that she's seen variations of this scene played out countless times. "Was this the guy?" I ask, hold out the snapshot from my desk.

"Maybe. We get lots of guys hocking heirlooms. Your brother, eh? Let me see that picture again. Nice-looking. But skinny, ain't he? I think I remember him — he had a nice voice." She sighs and flips open a ledger on the counter in front of her. Rifles through pages. "Gave him three hundred."

"Thanks. I appreciate it." Neither Cory nor Pockface profited much on their ends of the deal.

I leave the clerk in her cage and wander through the store, picking up and setting down detritus from other broken families. No one plans on pawn shops. The display window is filled with guitars, mostly Yamahas, bashed-up road warriors that my brother would disdain on his good days. One, cherrywood under a layer of peeling red paint, sounds resonant when I strum it. I am taken by its jaunty strap, pink leather edged with silky tassels. The clerk is watching me, her lips pursed. "It's a workhorse," she says, her eyebrows climbing.

"How much?"

"It's been here six months. Fifty bucks, and I'll throw in a music stand."

I laugh and leave, my hands empty.

Two weeks after I bought back the mandolin, the waitresses are jangling the clean cutlery and Jon is checking inventory with the bartender. Billy Cowsill's raucous cover of "I'm Movin' On" blares through the sound system, and I don't hear Rusty's knock at my office door. "Got a minute, Lise?" He's almost shouting. I tilt my head toward the chair. He closes the door. "Can I . . . ?" I nod as he picks up the mandolin from its stand. He moves his fingers, and frills flow from the strings, lace and satin notes. He smiles, holds it across his chest, one hand stroking the wood. "Bart says it used to belong to Bill Monroe. That true?" I nod again, watching him closely. He's trimmed his hair into a sleek helmet. When he takes a seat, his hands smooth an orbit on the sleeves of his black jacket, the nails tidy half-moons. He takes a deep breath. "Listen, Lise, about that bottle of Scotch. I was way out of line."

"Yeah. You were. Bygones. But no repeats, Rusty."

"Right. Just so's you know, I'm grateful. And it's Nathan. Anything I can do — "

I wave him out, notice the set of his angular shoulders as he replaces the mandolin on the stand. He's more like Jon than I gave him credit for.

An hour later, the house is full. Rusty and Bart are onstage and I am leaning on the counter, my coffee cooling as I listen to their harmonies. Something's changed. Rusty's voice sounds assured and his hands are steady on the strings. I look away from the band, surveying the audience, when a familiar pony-tail tracks a zigzag path through the crowded room. Jon reaches Cory at the same time I do, and says what I no longer dare to think.

"Cory, you look good, man. Clean. Come to make some music?"

"I'm good, man," Cory lightly punches Jon's shoulder, then laughs as I fling my arms around him.

"I'll just check the kitchen," Jon murmurs. I don't hear him leave.

"Let me get a look at you, Lise." Cory disentangles me, ruffles my short hair. "You're lookin' skinny. What did you do to your hair?"

"Cory, I wish you'd — "

"I'm okay, Lise. Brunette suits you."

I walk around him, scan his clothes, skin, face. Resist the urge to pat. My brother stands patiently under my scrutiny. He's looked worse. A new scar runs in a taut red crescent from one blond eyebrow to his hairline, but his jeans are clean and his cowboy boots are polished. Part of me wants to know where he's been sleeping and who's washing his clothes, but I don't ask. And I don't want to ask the other question, the invisible elephant. But it is pulled from my mouth like a rotting tooth. "Cory — "

"Lise. Just . . . don't."

I fumble for my puffer, but I left it on my desk. I wheeze into my sleeve and try to breathe gently. Ask anyway. "Where have you been?"

"Vancouver," he says flatly. Nothing else, just a few words and a tight smile for Sonya when she comes to take his order. When the cook's bell rings, I brush her away and bring his Reuben myself. He eats rapidly, methodically, head bent to the job, not looking up, forearms protecting his plate. When did he last eat three squares in a day? He feels my eyes on him, half-looks sideways at me, drops his gaze to his fries. When I stretch out my hand for his empty plate, he shakes his ponytail sharply and carries it into the kitchen himself before we edge down the crowded hall to my office.

"Why didn't you let me know where you were?"

"You're my sister, Lise. Not my mother. It's my own mess."

My face stings as if he has slapped me. I imagine I can hear the quivering strings of the Gibson and wonder what Mom would say to him. What she said to our father, the long-dead junkie and sax player we never met. The answer — for Cory, at least — is obvious, the same answer our aunt Crista has given him for years: get clean. The rest, I'll never know.

"Cory, about the mandolin." I stop. For half a minute, I waver. Maybe I shouldn't tell Cory. Re-string it. Learn to play it myself. My chest constricts. I'm not the musician. Cory is.

"Yeah. Broke my heart to sell it. But I've got three weeks clean. I'm going to meetings every day."

"Yeah, right."

"I told you, I'm clean. But I owe a guy two grand — "

"Again?" I can't keep the sarcasm from my voice. But Cory ignores the interruption.

" — and I wonder if — "

"What? Another loan? You know I don't like . . . "

"I know. But Lise, this guy really scares me." His face is white.

"All right. I've got cash in the safe at home. But Cory, look." I hesitate, then haul the Gibson from its cave between the filing cabinets. Cory's face softens. He hugs me, then picks up his mandolin, his face bent to its strings. It hums in his arms. "You could have all the work you want as a session player, Cory. I've got bands in here two mornings a week, laying down CD tracks. They'd all jump to have you."

"Sure thing. Sure." His eyes are on the mandolin in his hands as he tunes it. He doesn't ask me how I found it.

I've given up examining the ways and means my brother's life could have been. But when I hear the rippling opening notes of "Cotton Eyed Joe" pour from that beautiful instrument, my breath stops. I hide behind a cough.

We were seven when Mom heard a hint of what Cory could become. I went to lessons too, and tried not to flinch when every teacher ignored me after hearing my brother play. My asthma started at ten, and Mom, sighing, offered me painting classes. But no, I wanted to be with Cory, and bit back my wheezing while he practised chords and arpeggios. At thirteen, he graduated to Monroe's mandolin and I stopped pretending. I read his superhero comic books, one hand on my inhaler, while he played. Cory was obsessed, but he always asked me to play with him. I think about that generosity. It still feels bigger than my own greed for what he's thrown away.

Mom loved to sing with Cory. He wound harmonies around her contralto like ivy on a rosebush. When they sang, I dropped whatever I was doing and stood behind him, hugging him, my forehead against his back, my hands open on his chest to feel the vibrations in his body. Thought of ways to force the music to make the leap through the air into me. Ray guns. X-ray eyes. Nothing worked.

He wanted to tour with her, to all the places she'd sang in before we were born — Austin, Nashville, New Orleans, where she met my father playing in a jazz club on Decatur Street — and that little place in Tennessee where she found Monroe's mandolin. But he never got the chance. And I was glad, in some tautly closed part of me — not that Mom died, especially of the big C — but that Cory had been denied a small piece of what I couldn't have, and what Mom lost. When she lost both breasts, she quit singing. Said her breasts covered where her soul lived.

Aunt Crista hugged us as we stood beside the casket. Mom's white skin gleamed like her Meissen porcelain. I reached out and touched a cheek. Cold and smooth. The stillness of her deflated chest was visceral after the hospital, where we had been buried among harried nurses and blinking lights, forbidden to touch dials or adjust more than blanket and pillow.

Cory sang "Satan's Jewel Crown" during the service. Just him and that mandolin. When the final notes faded from the strings, he laid his head on the lectern. No one in the congregation drew a breath until I got up, took his arm and led him back in the silence to our pew.

It's been ten years since the first time I went looking for him. Cory's cleaned himself up a dozen times. He comes and goes. I never know which man may show up — the stranger, lost in a chemical haze, or my brother the musician, eager to play.

The phone wakes me. Crista's weekly call. "Yes, he was here. No sign of him," I tell her, peering into the guest room. The bed is rumpled but empty. I sigh. "I gave him some money last night."

I hold the receiver away from my ear as Crista's voice twangs into the room. " — in god's name did you do that, Lise? You know he'll — " I listen with half an ear as my aunt berates me, then cut her off.

"I don't regret it. Damn it, Crista, we've been through this before." Her voice winds down after a few minutes.

His voice and mandolin were the last sounds I had heard last night as I drifted off, wound together in a lullaby that soothed me straight back to childhood. But this morning, as I make coffee, I try not to think about debts or threats, but I feel a widening within my chest, as if an umbilical cord has loosened. Jon asked me once why I never send a private investigator to find my brother when he disappears. Too steep a price, I told him curtly. Ransoming the mandolin, and its disappearance so soon after, is another pair of waves sent toward a distant coast. We live on separate continents, my twin and me. I can bail him out forever, send wave after wave towards that invisible shore, or I can stop. Direct the current into my own life.

On my way to work, I wheel the Jeep west through the crowded traffic along 16th Avenue, and pull into the parking lot at Sharky's. Sitting there, winter sunlight ice-pale around me, I can imagine Jon's derisive voice when he learns what I am contemplating. I look down at my hands. In my inner ear, I hear the sea's melody coursing, and as I walk into the pawn shop, I am suddenly, soberly, sure.

I'll ask Rusty to teach me to play, finally begin my own apprenticeship. Jon would appreciate that. Maybe Cory will too, and maybe he'll never notice.

I leave Sharky's with the red guitar's battered case and a music stand bumping and kissing around the backs of my knees like shy teenagers on the beach.

Nerve

From my perch along the rail, I can't fault the start of Hailey's dressage test — smooth halt, precise nodding salute to the judges. But the bloody girl's torso is so stiff, I'm completely surprised when Rumi glides into the half-paused aria of a collected trot. Then I see Hailey's backbone ease into her saddle, and my own body relaxes, too. Maybe they'll be fine. Maybe. She nudges Rumi into a canter and I'm momentarily lulled. But a minute later, she inexplicably pulls him to a halt in front of the judges' table. Bloody hell. She must have forgotten the next movement. I can just imagine what Stan will have to say about this. Her pop's down at the gate, doing a slow burn, scattering cigarette ashes as the clerk reads the next movement, his measured voice loud enough for the whole stadium to hear. Watching Hailey's flushed face as she listens, I wonder where I buried my old top hat. If I can find it, it would do her more justice than that faded helmet she wears, give her a little dignity.

The ride goes downhill from there. Hailey's definitely rattled, and after her closing salute, heading out of the ring, she takes a quick sliding glance at her father, dismay written all over her face. Six months of schooling and hard work down the tube. But she's got spunk, and recovers in time to give Nate a quick thumbs-up just as his crazy mare shies at the nodding lilies edging the ring. Hailey's just sixteen. It must be hard for her not to feel envious of Nate; at twenty-three, he seems unflappable, even during their group jumping lessons when everything that mare does goes to sixes and sevens.

My cane catches in the sand as I hobble toward the barn, hoping to reach her ahead of Stan. I'm not surprised she hasn't asked about my limp. She's so obviously used to a whiphand, she likely expects I'd unleash my "none of your bloody business" glare on her. Six months ago, I would have. Not now. This girl doesn't need another cutting-down.

But if I unloaded a few well-chosen bricks on her pop's head and ditch him as a paying customer, who'll look out for her and Rumi?

I first met them when they drove out to my ranch late last autumn to inquire about lessons. As Stan swung out of his truck, I noticed his fingernails, edged in black, his denim shirt straining across his torso, his narrow-lipped mouth pulled tight. I knew right away that he was a man I'd not be too eager to cross, certainly not what my old Ma would have called "a fine upstanding gentleman."

His first words to me: "That fence could use some paint." I shrugged it off, my eye on the gawky goosegirl behind him, her long neck retreating at his tone as she unloaded her horse, a spanky penny-bright Arab with a dishy face and wide white blaze. "I worked as a stablehand as a kid back in Ontario," he said, watching his daughter tack up. "Mucked out more'n enough stalls. I had enough of shovelling it. It's time to be the guy at the bridle end collecting the trophies." I told him we'd see right enough about that.

My ranch is a modest one, twenty acres of hillside north of Cochrane, perched above the Ghost River, complete with a tiny leaky house and a cranky gas range, a stony garden, and an airy hip-roofed barn. The hills swoop past the barn; coyotes, deer and a fearless mother skunk with three kits all regularly emerge from the coulees to investigate my yard. I adore the place, and I've sweated like a navvy so it — and I — can earn our keep. I walk the entire fence line every day to check on my lame boarders, Molly and Pistachio, both retired racehorses, out grazing on the north slope's spring fescue. If they were mine, I'd shoot both and buy some young stock with promise, but their board pays a big bite of the rent.

Recently, my landlord's been making noises about selling, and now the grumpy old bugger's close to putting a bill of sale on the table. Ma's bit of cash will just cover the down payment, but the rest is up to me. It's been five Canadian winters since Ethan left me. Since I left England. I thought I'd gotten over missing riding, but when my back aches in winter, I remember all too acutely how it feels to ride a horse's arcing spine en route to heaven, life stretching toward the infinite, the unexplainable, the incalculable. Living in those silent hills feels like compensation for what I've lost.

By the time I reach the stable, Hailey has ditched her helmet and jacket in the manger. She eases Rumi's bridle over his ears, slips his halter into place and bends her face to nuzzle his cheeks without a word. Well, at least she's not crying. Lord knows I howled the first time I forgot a test.

Her father pushes past me and grabs the bridle. He fills the aisle, shaking the bit in hands as broad as a Percheron's hooves.

"Stan," I say, making bloody sure my tone is at even keel, "we all forget a test at one time or other. Goes with the territory. I'll handle this."

"I'm the one footing the tab. Kindly step out of my way, Coralie, so I can talk to my daughter."

"I'll thank you to be keeping a civil tone. *And* keep your voice down. I'll not have you upsetting the horses, too."

He turns his back and drops the decibels, but it's sharpened by that edge I first heard when he set foot on my ranch, the sarcasm of a poor man who likes what he sees and can't figure out how to have it for himself. "Hailey, you've disappointed me. Your one job was to memorize the damn test."

Hailey leans on Rumi's far side, her horse a shield, her face hidden against his ribs. Her shoulders start to heave. With nowhere else to look that won't embarrass her, I pluck her jacket and helmet from the manger, brush off the oats and hay, and stare at Stan's workboots, their steel toes gleaming through the worn leather.

Stan's voice drops even more, and I have to lean in to hear him. "Coralie says you've got promise. If you're not going to take this seriously, I'll sell the horse." He holds out the bridle without looking at me, drops it, stalks away. The bit cracks against my elbow. I keep my back turned as I hang the bridle on its hook, just in case Hailey needs a wee bit of what these Canadians so blandly call "space." When I turn around, her skin has lost a little of the grey tightness around the eyes that settles into her every time Stan is around. She lifts her face from Rumi's coat. The gelding whickers and nudges at her arm.

"Odds are he doesn't mean it, Hailey."

"Yes, he does," she says. "He's a bully."

"He is that." A terrible thought occurs to me, and I study her covertly, wondering. Surely not.

She reads my mind. "He's never hit me, if that's what you're wondering."

"Let it go, girl. Julia's on deck. Let's go watch her ride." My words sound lame even to me, and Hailey's silent rebuff skewers me as we leave the stable.

Julia's performance is flawless. She's a natural. Everything's easy for her, I suspect, her life a non-stop curve of ups and dipsy-doodles without the emotional elevator falls that Hailey endures. Julia's blonde ponytail can always be spotted at the centre of a group of riders drinking coffee and comparing notes. Her family is old Alberta money, and her custom-made jacket, its red-lined tail flipping in the breeze, cost ten times what I spend on oats each month.

Julia exits the ring, leaning forward in her saddle and hugging her mare's dappled neck, her breeches snug over her arse. Mindful of the younger girl, still sniffling, standing at my shoulder, I simply nod in acknowledgement as Julia halts her mare, pulls off her top hat and shakes out her hair while listening to Nate's analysis of her test, and I fiddle with the program in my hands.

"Why doesn't your mother come along?" I ask Hailey *sotto voce*, and immediately kick myself for my obtuseness.

Hailey's face screws up. "Work. She gets a shift premium for working nights at the hospital. She sleeps days."

Her mother didn't come to the previous competition last month either, a brilliant blue June afternoon in the foothills near

Priddis, just beyond Calgary's southernmost suburbs. Hailey and Rumi got lost on the cross-country course and were eliminated. That's not so unusual for a novice, but you'd have thought the world had come to a bloody crashing end, the way Stan carried on. He wouldn't look at his daughter, and it was me who finally helped her bandage Rumi's legs at the afternoon's end. Hailey was hunched like an old deckhand as she loaded him into the trailer. As they drove away, she stared out the passenger window, her face bleak. I imagine that the silence lasted all the way to my barn and along the winding highway to their home in northwest Calgary.

Mothering is not on the books along with teaching. I've got more than enough on my own plate — I don't want to get tangled in those lives, no matter how much I sympathize with the girl, who's obviously drawn the short straw in the father category. I place my hand on Hailey's shoulder, neutral territory, and summon up my best Brit-backbencher tone. "Let it go, girl. You've got the cross-country to think about next. Find a quiet spot to review your map. I'll go check on the horses."

Stan waylays me as I pass his camper en route to the barn, a cigarette clenched between those tight lips.

"Stan, you can't smoke here."

He stubs the match under his boot, puffing unrepentantly. "Keep her head in the game, Coralie. I've got plans for that horse, maybe even the Olympics eventually if that kid can keep her wits about her. A gold medal in the china cabinet would be just the ticket."

"You're joking, surely. She's a novice, and Rumi is no international-level horse. That calibre of animal would set you back thousands and thousands! And Hailey may never — "

He cuts me off. "So maybe not the Olympics, but I put in a double shift every day last month, plumbing that new subdivision on the west side to pay for this little jaunt. She's damn well gonna stick with it."

"You can't expect her to redeem your childhood, Stan. She's just a kid."

"Kids are supposed to make their parents proud, Coralie. That's what I'm payin' you for. You don't want the job? I'll find someone else."

There. He's played his trump card. "You're pushing too hard, Stan. Let her scratch. She's nerved out."

"No. Absolutely not."

We're in the barn when the announcer reads out the standings, metallic echoes chipping corners off the rafters. Julia stands second and Nate is a respectable sixth. Hailey is in a clutch near the bottom, tied for sixteenth.

Sympathetic Nate gets there ahead of me. "Don't sweat it, kiddo," he says gently from the adjacent stall. "You've got more events ahead. We all have off days."

"You're lucky your dad is so interested in your riding, Hailey," Julia calls from Astral's stall. "Maybe he'd like to walk the course with us." Talk about tactless. All that money hasn't taught her anything about how fragile the human heart really is. I ought to take her aside for a serious girl-talk.

Nate, watching Hailey's face, quickly interjects. "Hailey's dad told me earlier that he's not walking it."

I turn back to Hailey, on her knees beside her horse, a brush in her hand. When she starts a tuneless humming, he drops his head to hers, and she reaches blindly to stroke his muzzle. It's a tender sight, and I feel a slight whiffle of relief — at least she has Rumi to love.

"Hailey," I say, conscious of sounding like a drone, "pay attention to what's at hand. Do you want to finish this competition?" She won't look at me, her attention fixed on Rumi, stroking his shins gently. Finally she nods without looking up. It's not the wholehearted "Yes!" I had hoped for, but it's better than a flat denial. "All right then." I turn to my other students. "Grab a sandwich and your rainjackets. I'll meet you in the yard."

Straw rustles as they leave the stable. Hailey rubs her nose. She looks pale. I take her arm and lead her to a secluded stall. "Sit down on this bale. Catch your breath. In a few minutes, we'll just — "

"Get on with it?"

"Yes. Exactly. We'll just get on with it." I shrug and gently tap Hailey's forehead with my forefinger. "Life is never fair, Hailey. It's rarely even halfway bloody decent. I learned that the hard way from my old Ma."

As I briskly rub her cold hand, an echoing numbness runs through my pelvis and my thigh, just as it had that rainy day at Aintree, when Ma's stallion, Austin, clipped a rail. Flipped in mid-air. Landed on me, smashed my thigh bone. My knee was — well, everyone knows how I walk. I'll never ride again, and I can't have kids, something happened to my pelvis. Ma always said they should have put me down and let the damned horse live. She blamed me until they put her in her grave. And Stan is almost as cold a bugger.

"You have to grow some backbone, girl. It's your life, not his."

"Your old Ma and my Dad would have made a fine pair."

It's the first show of humour she's mustered all afternoon. "No doubt. Now let's go walk the course."

Stan is at the barn door, studying the immaculate white and green fences edging the paddocks. Hailey ducks away as he beckons.

"You go on ahead, Hailey," I tell her. "I won't be a minute. Stan, a word. Then I have to walk the course with the girls and Nate."

"Ah, relax. Ya got plenty of time. This is the life, eh, Coralie? What I want for Hailey." He nods at the buildings. "I know rich folks. I saw how they live, back east. Like this." He nudges me and winks. "You need to get yourself a rich man, Coralie. Then you could fix up that plain-Jane bit you rent. Start your own string. Maybe build an outfit like this. That's what it takes — horses, and land. Money. Hailey's gotta learn that."

"Money? That's the worst reason to have a horse, Stan. That's not the reason your girl rides."

He makes a pawing motion, as if halfway considering a grab at my arm, but thinks better of it. "About this afternoon. Maybe my kid can gain some ground, right?"

"Stan, Hailey will be lucky to finish the course. You should let her — "

"What, quit? Balls. No one gets anywhere by quitting. Speaking of, that gelding has balls enough for both of them." He turns away, lighting the next cigarette.

As I head toward my waiting students, I ponder the unanswerable. How does he sleep at night? That cold, voracious appetite. Then I remember the one decent thing my mother did for me, and my face burns. Land. I want the deed to my little bit of hillside. My inheritance adds up to a tidy down payment on my own appetite.

Walking the course gives me a chance to settle my thoughts, although Hailey grumbles at the first fence, a bullfinch, its low wooden frame stuffed with scraggy shrubbery in full yellow flower. We pace twelve strides from the bullfinch to a narrow railway barrier, a dangling triangle, all air and red stripes. A bent jackpine as a landmark at the turn off the track. Then a sloppy stack of bales and a stone wall, its pillars festooned with orange kite tails.

Halfway through the course, Nate peers over a split rail fence perched on the lip of the ridge. "Blitz is gonna love this drop," he says. Beyond it, the track plunges down the belly of an old gravel pit.

Hailey's face whitens, and in that instant, I decide where to position myself to watch my students as they ride the course. "What's this?" she cries in despair, gesturing at the tangled thickets of wild roses that line the narrow path below us.

I look squarely at her, inject steel into my voice. "These fences are no bigger than what you've been schooling Rumi over, just different shapes. Do you want to scratch?"

"I can't scratch, Coralie. My father would never forgive me."

When we return to the yard, I catch her staring at the plywood map posted on the barn wall.

"If you think too much about falling, you'll fall for sure. Look past the jump, to where you want to land. It's like the bullfinch, Hailey, a leap of faith."

"All I can see is Rumi falling."

"He won't. Not if you approach the jump properly. Not if you trust him."

Her hands are shaking as she turns away.

It is raining steadily by the time the first horse heads on course. Stan, an enormous yellow slicker draped serape-style over one shoulder, stalks off to find a viewpoint without a word to Hailey. I am glad to see him go; anything he might say could only make things worse.

"Don't rush your fences," I murmur, holding Rumi by his bridle while Hailey mounts. "You have lots of time." I hand her a pair of gloves. "You'll need these. Be brave." When Hailey pulls the crumpled map from her breeches pocket, I crinkle my nose and wink. "You know the route, Hailey. Trust yourself."

Hailey's half-laugh almost reassures me until I hear the quaver in her voice as Rumi tries to shy. "Cut it out, Rumi!" She kicks him into a canter, circles, comes back and halts beside me. I should have scratched her entry myself, and the devil take the hindmost. Too late now. "I know what you're thinking," she says, "but I'm not doing this for him. I'm doing it for Rumi. He deserves this chance."

"Bravo." I hold up two thumbs as she trots away, but I simply don't believe her. Not after watching her with Stan for the past six months. My mouth fills, the black metal of empathy. I'd ride the course for her if I could.

A deep-chested black leaps over the warm-up jump, with Rumi five strides back. At the start line, the black bursts into a gallop and heads for the first fence.

Three minutes later, the starter's air-pistol barks and Hailey moves Rumi across the line at a canter. I watch long enough to see him sail through the bullfinch's gaping blossoms, then pull my head in like a turtle's and limp down the spectators' shortcut to the bottom of the quarry. I'll have to hurry to watch Hailey take the drop fence. Should have scratched her. Should have. I am abruptly aware of the cold raindrops dripping from my beret onto my neck. At the stone wall, its kites flickering like Chinese dragons, I see Stan perched on a rock. He waves as I limp past to the split rail, then edge down the hillside. When I reach the viewing spot at its base, my heart is pounding and my leg aches. By the time I catch my breath, the black horse ahead of Hailey skids down the slope, his rider bent double over his neck.

I look up the hill at the sound of Hailey's raised voice. "Come on, Rumi! You can do it!"

An ominous double-beat rattle, Rumi's hooves, catching the top rail. I see him, silhouetted against the sky, arcing over the fence, and Hailey, shaken loose, a rag-doll against his withers.

Rumi's shoulders crumple, his hind heels cartwheel overhead, and they somersault down the hill. Gravity pulls Hailey inexorably out of the saddle. As she falls free and rolls, I see again the thrashing legs of my mother's stallion, scrabbling and panicking as he fell. My pelvis throbs, just as it had, hot and cold by turn.

When Hailey hits the quarry's bottom, a deadfall of blackened logs halts her momentum. Rumi lands on his side, jammed against a clump of aspens. I lurch through the loose gravel and sand toward Hailey, swearing with each step. When I reach her, Hailey's eyes are closed although tears are spilling down her cheeks. Her entire left leg is buried under the deadfall. Blood drips from her nose onto her gloves.

The fence judge runs up behind me from the observers' station and grabs my arm. "Don't touch her!"

Hailey opens her eyes, spits out a mouthful of blood and stares around her. In her face, I see the exact moment when she realizes what has happened. "Rumi!" He lifts his head at the sound of her voice and whickers, foam and blood splattering his chest and the leaves under his neck.

Crouching beside her, I whisper. "Hailey. Can you hear me?" She barely nods. "This man will help you. I'll see to Rumi." I leave her under the close eye of the official and hobble the ten feet to Rumi, kneel beside him, take his bridle and lay his head down on the dirt. He grunts, then sighs. His front legs are crossed like an old granny's at tea, one shin buckling at an odd double angle, sure evidence of a compound fracture. "Get the vet!"

The walkie-talkie crackles. I swivel and watch the jump judge gently brush Hailey's face clean, a cloth blotting the blood beneath her nose, his grey raincoat draped over her. It should be her father beside her, tending her, but he's nowhere in sight. Within me, anger lights its quick fuse, a spark against the long burn of guilt. I shove both down. Later will be enough time to face what needs facing.

"Hailey, I'm over here with Rumi." I see her shudder. "Cry if you need to. Swear like a sailor, damn it. It might help. I'll be right there, just soon as the vet — " Soon enough will be too soon for her, so I clench back the rest of the words, think about my mother. Her stiff upper lip that held me far from her.

The rain slows. Blood puddles on the ground beneath Rumi's jaw. He lies quietly, his ears stilled, his ribs slowly moving, my hand smoothing his neck, hypnotically stroking. The sound of running footsteps doesn't rouse him, but Hailey murmurs as the vet hurries down the same path I had followed.

He looks at me questioningly. "You okay to help?" At my nod, he extends a hand and I scramble to my feet. He scowls as he stares at the downed horse. "We'll have to roll him clear of the trees. Grab his hooves on that side. Ready? On my count." I cup two black hooves in my hands. "One. Two. Roll!" The saddletree cracks. Rumi's scream is almost human. The vet touches my arm. "I'll be back in a minute. I left my rifle in the truck."

"My horse!" Hailey's voice wavers behind me.

I drop to my knees beside Rumi and flatten my palms against his long cheekbones, gather my breath and pray, long slow seconds of losing myself, this is not what I want, god, not what I want, god don't let this happen to her too, not on my watch. I had forgotten that I knew how. Under my hands, Rumi's breath flutters. I slow my inhalations, try to sense his breathing slowing with me. Several minutes pass, and I am lightheaded when I manage to look at Hailey.

Two paramedics have arrived, and set a stretcher on the ground beside her. One buries a needle in her arm. "Sorry, miss. This'll help." He nods to the jump judge, who pries the deadfall off her leg with a metal bar.

The vet returns and brusquely tugs my arm. "Step back." I retreat. At Hailey's side, stumbling over the stretcher handle, I drop my cane and crouch at her shoulder, take her hand, her bloody glove limp between my fingers. Behind us, the dull click of cartridges chambering into the vet's rifle.

"Hailey," I say. "Look at me. Don't watch."

In the silence, I hear the whisper of raindrops on leaves, clods of dirt and a sifting of wet sand trickling down the hillside. Hailey's gaze slides past my face. I turn my head, tracking her sightline as she watches Stan skid down the hill. His eyes are fixed not on his daughter, but on the vet, sighting down the barrel of his rifle. I try to pray again, but my prayers are all about me, my little piece of land, my days on its hillside. After the bullet has worked its mercies, I know with hard, bare certainty that I will ream Stan with words like the harshest spurs, then walk away from him. But not from this broken girl with the dim light of hospitals and horses in her eyes.

The hand in mine convulsively tightens. All her longing coalesces, then her face pinches closed, as plain to read as light on leaves. "Hailey," I whisper. "You'll go riding again. In the hills behind my barn. No fences, no jumping. Just you and the horses."

The Good Husband

"I HAVE TWO CHOICES," GEORGE TELLS me, then he lights another smoke. A cigarette is constantly in his mouth, except for when he carries Trudy in and out of her garden. Her litany of illnesses over the last two years is long, from female complaints to irritable bowel. She doesn't need carrying but he persists, the habit formed after her accident, a fall from the stage that wrenched her life into its present narrow shape. Trudy slid from painkillers to this other form of dependence that would have made my Astrid weep to witness.

We are drinking coffee in my back yard, sitting in the chairs that Astrid painted, oranges and pinks splattered over a solid teal background. "What do you mean, two choices?" I say.

"You know. Faithful. Or not."

"C'mon, George, marriage is more complicated than that." Then I stop to reflect.

Trudy lives in a shabby blue bathrobe. I doubt if she combs her hair from one day to the next. When I pass through my gate adjoining their yard, she waves half-heartedly. I rarely hear her voice anymore, and her movements have faded to a shuffle. Seems like she has settled permanently into her starring role as an invalid. She was a jazz dancer, the full grace of God in her arms, legs, even her hands. A torso rippling with muscles, platinum hair to her waist. Watching her was like watching a river. Before her accident, she choreographed and performed a one-woman show that Astrid and George and I attended at the Arts Centre, a torrential event of charged sexuality. She and George came over after the show's premiere. Trudy was still high, and swept Astrid around the kitchen in a spinning waltz that had George and me dumbstruck. "There's no room in art for milquetoast," she said as I poured the champagne. Now she shuffles, and seems older than Astrid was when she died.

"No, you're right, George," I say and sip my coffee, "it isn't complicated after all. You're in or you're out. But the choice should be easy, man. Treasure her. Each day is a gift." As I say it, I remember my sunlit final days with Astrid. The pain of losing her is still there. Morning and evening, I stumble over missing moments. I can't get used to their echo.

George lights another cigarette and ponders. "Why would a middle-aged couple meet in a parking lot?" he finally asks, squirming.

Another breath-held morning. Astrid's perennials are in bloom, sprawling across the beds, climbing the fence. It's been three years. Those flowers are almost unbearable. Last spring, I swore I'd rip out the beds and put down gravel, but they remind me of her. So Dina, our neighbour Lorraine's daughter, weeds the beds for me. She's a university student, still at home. She brings lemonade in the evenings, and we share it when she's finished sweating and digging, just as Astrid and I used to. This house rattles with thirty years of memories.

"C'mon, George, there's lots of reasons for people to meet in a parking lot."

"That park near the Stampede grounds we visited the year Astrid was so stuck on rock gardens, that parking lot. Walking through it last week, I saw a couple there, way past middle-aged, he had grey hair and a limp. They got out of two cars, and ran to meet each other. Like kids. They had their hands all over each other . . ."

I'm starting to wonder. Has George been getting some action while Trudy's been so sick? It's been two years since her accident.

"Alex, did you and Astrid stop — you know? When she was so sick." George and I have talked about many things over the years, but sex has never been one of them. But here he is blushing like a teenager. "Never mind, I didn't mean to pry."

He stubs out his cigarette and leans across the table. His belly juts against the chair's arm. George manages a supermarket in the south end of town. He used to be a produce buyer for the chain, travelling to China, California, Chile, visiting farms and looking for perfect fruit and vegetables. Since Trudy's illness, he gets no farther than pacing the produce department. A lot of weight has accumulated, mentally and physically.

"At work," he says, sounding sheepish, "there's this jock in marketing, his wife's a hot babe. He hangs out at the gym, talks about the old days, football, mostly, being the quarterback, all that. But lately he's been talking about — well, chat rooms and sex in motels, and in his car, and in the sales room once, for chrissakes, a blow job. Some woman was *under* the table, kneeling between the sample cases of organic apples. I walked in with a stack of orders in my hand and her ass was front and centre. Sex is all he has on his mind. He says his wife won't put out now that she's pregnant."

"George. What's this go to do with you and Trudy? Wait a sec . . . You haven't, have you? Have you?"

His silence is answer enough.

Well, who am I to judge? Although I never did step out on Astrid, I did my share of looking. And before we met, there was this one woman, a dancer like Trudy. I met her in my last year at university, the year I wrote my first play. We used to meet backstage after rehearsals. What she could do with her legs would make a contortionist envious.

"I couldn't help it," says George, looking hangdog. "Once. A woman from my gym. The only time I can touch Trudy anymore is when I help her in or out of bed. Or carry her out here. And that damn dressing gown, well, you've seen it, Alex, it's all she'll wear. I'd lie down and die for her if she'd just — "

I drink my coffee. The silence lengthens. George walks into my kitchen, brings back the carafe, pours us each another mug. He hands me the brown sugar. I keep my eyes on the coffee I'm stirring. The spoon goes round and round the mug without clinking.

"The worst of it is the pills. Her doc has her on this bizarre cocktail, and she's either sleeping or drugged to the eyeballs, and when she's doped up she says the most god-awful things."

"What do you mean? Trudy's a sweetie."

"She is. But she keeps saying she's had enough. And then she shuts up and cries. Between that and no . . . Well, like I said. I was at the gym — "

"George! Stop, for crying out loud. I don't want to hear the details."

"I gotta tell somebody, man. I can't stand myself, and she's so sick."

When I look up, Trudy is standing just inside my yard.

George nearly trips as he rushes over to her. "Hey, sweetie, come sit down. How's your head today?"

She murmurs so quietly he bends his head to hear.

"Are you sure?"

She nods.

"All right then. Alex, Trudy is wondering if you'd like to come for lunch. Saturday."

I haven't been inside their house since Trudy's fall. Looking through their window is as close as I have gotten. I flounder a bit, trying to figure out the sea change.

"Um. You sure you're up to it? "

She smiles, a ghost of the old Trudy. George wraps one arm around her waist as they leave my yard. I'm relieved to see them go. Our houses almost touch, kitchen windows eye to eye, side-by-side back decks, our glass balconies practically kissing on the upper floor. I see and hear so much of their lives as it is, I feel like a card-carrying voyeur. George's exposure is more than I can stand. Astrid and I had a habit of silence, me engrossed in my current play, her reading the latest Mavis Gallant or flipping through the *New Yorker*. Sharp humour instead of histrionics. Control in spades, most of the time.

When Astrid got so ill so quickly, solicitude came easily: we both knew she'd come home to die, we had made that promise, that we'd not let the other die in a hospital bed. But not so soon. She was only fifty-three. She was still keeping the interns on their toes at the law firm.

The ambulance drivers set her gently in our double bed, her oxygen tubes carefully arranged. When they left, I stretched out beside her and put my arms around her as if she was bone china.

"Come on, Alex. Really hold me," she said. Not briskly, but matter-of-fact. So I made love to her, doing my best to ignore the tubes and the oxygen tank, wondering how many more times I'd embrace her. She was home for a week. She had been sleeping, a long mid-afternoon nap with the blinds wide open to the sun, and I had crawled under the duvet to cradle her long body against me. She never woke. I was grateful it had been so peaceful for her. But I wish I'd had more mornings to bring her breakfast in the garden and make her lunch. Her absence is not just a hole in my life. It's my life, ending too, on a slow winding path back to her garden.

The next morning, over coffee on the upstairs balcony, I see George pour Trudy's tea, and I hear his cowboy boots follow her when she meanders out of my sight. Their voices are as clear as if they were sitting here, not two walls removed.

"Here, sweetie. Eat some melon, you liked it last week. Try it?"

Cutlery clatters, then her slippers shush past the back door onto the deck. She avoids looking up at me, and the waft of tobacco floats by.

The sun is still high when he comes home from work with a full grocery bag. An hour later, I'm fixing a drink in the kitchen to the heavy scent of grilling steaks and smoke drifting from his grill. Although George says she barely eats, Trudy's belly is puffy, distended by the dope her doctor has her on. But while George's attention is fixed on the grill, I see her hands, normally placid on her lap, fiddling with the steak knives and salt shaker. Her jaw is set, her eyebrows wrenched together with tension. A while later, the steak on her plate goes to the kitchen untouched.

At two AM, I'm settled in a comforter on Astrid's old divan on the balcony, moon-watching. Coyotes, madrigals in four part harmony, the late night sky ruffled with melody. My hair damp against my neck. Downstairs and through the glass doors, George is clearly visible. His bulky shape is outlined through the lace curtains, his back to me as he stands at the counter with his hands in the sink. Cigarette smoke curling above his head. He doesn't look up, although I think by the set of his neck, he knows I am here. I'm puzzled. Trudy hasn't cooked in months. What has triggered her unexpected interest? Did she hear George's comments about her drugs? Or about his straying? Or neither? That seems hard to believe. This invitation is too abrupt to be coincidence. As I finish my mint tea, waiting to hear the coyotes again, I try to ignore the small sounds, perhaps sobbing, that filter through their kitchen window.

On Saturday morning, I'm drinking coffee on my deck when I see George leave the house. At eleven, Trudy hobbles through the glass doors and collapses in the chair beside the grill. She's in a sack-like grey dress that hides what has happened to her athlete's body. I avert my eyes, but she waves and whispers. I have to lean across the railing to hear.

"Dim sum, Alex."

Of course. Takeout from Chinatown.

During lunch, George leaps from the table every five minutes to bring out more dishes, a fresh pot of tea. "Shui mai?" He holds out the steamer basket filled with pork dumplings, but Trudy turns her face away. "Eel in tofu?" She shakes her head. He waves barbecued pork buns at her, then rice noodle pancakes. Nothing. "Trudy, honey, you love this stuff. What gives?" He slumps over his tea, lights a cigarette and studies the cherry trees.

I am acutely anxious for him, and scathingly angry with Trudy. Time to leave before I betray my feelings. As I turn to go, a hint of a smile, malicious and triumphant, arrows at me from Trudy, reclining in her chaise.

Astrid and I had the occasional blow-up. Every marriage does, and Astrid was used to being in charge. We lived in a careful bubble of acquiescence, me yielding, her biting her tongue. Unpredictable little things set her off, but she usually wrapped her irritation in wit. One afternoon when she was baking a cake for Stacey's birthday, I came into the kitchen, just to be friendly, and leaned against the cupboard watching her separate eggs and measure sugar in efficient movements.

"You going to stand there all day? Can't you make yourself useful?" She waved her arm toward the cupboard. "I need the cake pan. Get it down, will you?"

Cake pan found, I resumed my station. But something had gotten into her.

"For chrissakes, Alex. Don't just watch me. Do something."

"Astrid — " I took two steps toward her.

"Here. Separate this." She reached down to the carton of eggs on the counter, picked one up. Tossed it. Underhand, gently. To me. I put out my hand in sheer reflex, and caught it like a first baseman's lob to second. She threw another, laughing, then another. I managed to catch nearly all of them, but the last two got by me. It was either drop the six I was cradling or let them go by. They whistled past me, thudded dully on the cupboard door behind me. In amazement, I watched the eggs slide down the wall.

"Astrid! What was that all about?" She was weeping. "Honey, hush. It's okay."

I put my arms around her. When she finished, we washed the cupboard door and the floor. Astrid didn't speak until we sat down over a cup of tea. Her voice was tiny.

"Alex. Sorry. Sometimes I just want to shake you. I get tired of being the one who initiates everything."

I picked her up and carried her to bed.

Through the open window, I overhear George's gruff voice. "I don't want to fight, sweetie. You're not yourself. Those drugs . . . " He carries his coffee out to the balcony.

Trudy's voice follows him, a follow-up to her dim sum initiative. "I hate how you fuss over me, George. I can't stand it."

George, at the sink, has his back turned, but I see his body deflate.

"I want a divorce, George. No discussion. This is the me I am. Now. From now on."

He looks around, sees me on my balcony. I step indoors, move as far forward in the building as I can. I think about escape, about going into the garage, into the car, into the street, unrolling a few kilometres of insulation between us. He's not the type to detonate, but you never know, and George isn't quite the man I thought he was.

My car exits the driveway with a purr of the overhead door. In my rearview mirror, I see George's red Firebird on my tail as I roll around the corner. I pull over, unwind my window and lean out, but he stares straight in front of him and drives away.

George avoids me for a few days, his back turned whenever he's outside, the lace drawn between our houses like the Iron Curtain. I'm surprised, but not really. People like a scapegoat. I try not to take it personally, but I miss the company. He breaks the ice one sunny morning as I sit in my yard, an old copy of *Close Range* open on my lap.

"Morning."

"George, hey, how's things?"

"Got a light?"

"Yes, of course." We fuss with the matches. Each sputters and almost catches flame, then one spurts into a small blossom. His cigarette lit, he settles into the chair, easing his broad back into its curve. "How's Trudy?"

"In bed since you left the other day. I hoped it was a tempest in a teapot. She cried all day." He sighs and stares at the river valley. "But later, she asked if I'd been unfaithful. All I could think of was what if we stacked up all those cardboard dim sum takeaway boxes and swore to be faithful on top of them? It would be just as meaningful. I had to tell her. She kept at me all day, said she wanted to know, just couldn't leave it alone. You know what women are like." He catches himself, looks at me wryly. "Well, what *our* women are like."

My Astrid's face on the pillow, extinguished. I don't have the heart to correct him.

"So that's it, then."

"Yep. That's it. She's changed her mind twice. Now she says she's leaving."

The realtor hangs a For Sale sign on my fence in October, a week before he lists George and Trudy's house. Astrid's poppies are brown and toppled by frost in her garden, the towering sunflowers picked blind by birds. My writing is stalled, my days too long. George is jumpy, trying to quit smoking. It's too much, I tell him. Quit later. You can only handle what you can handle.

On a sun-glazed Indian summer day, doors and windows wide to catch the late warmth, I am packing up the front library when the door slams. Trudy, a silent shadow shuffling into a waiting cab. Two suitcases. I stand behind the curtains, watching. If Astrid was here, she'd make an acerbic observation about the folly of lovers and humanity in general. She wouldn't assign blame, so I don't either. I can hear George clinking glasses and ice cubes through the membrane of lace. I walk through her garden and up the back stairs. George meets me at the door. "She's gone to her sister's," he says, and hands me a whisky.

Neither of us is good at staying in touch. I get the occasional email, then one resigned note telling me they got back together again, but it fizzled. He goes back to travelling. I go back to writing, my computer on the dining room table in my new condo downtown, the river hidden by skyscrapers. Halfway through my new play, I see them clearly as I hunch over my keyboard, the two women in our kitchen, bright as poppies, and I feel the thin line of yearning for what I want the past to be. But I can't compel my typing past the grit of eggshells, the disdained pork dumplings. The women stay in my memory. The screen in front of me stays blank.

Still Life with Birds

Today, like every workday, begins in the restaurant kitchen. Without turning on the radio to break the lake's silence, Ariana makes a cheese and chive omelette for the two of them to share. Plates and espressos in hand, she climbs the back stairs and enters Violetta's bedroom without knocking.

"Vi. It's time."

"It's time to begin, isn't it," Vi warbles from her bed, deliberately off-key. Ariana has learned to interpret every blink of her sister's one functioning eye, and when Vi winks, she looks past the stare of the blind right iris, glazed wide open. Vi giggles, picks up her meter and tests her sugar levels. Ariana, perched on the foot of the bed, has to look away when Vi slides the needle into her upper arm.

They eat in silence. Ariana rolls the ties of Vi's yellow sunhat between her fingers and sips her coffee. Vi still surprises her, flashes of humour embedded like unexpected glass. She can see the lake through the window, smooth except for the ruffle of wild waterfowl along the shore. *Bonne anniversaire, ma belle,* she says to Violetta.

"Don't say it, Ariana. Please."

"Vi, we need to talk. You could have broken your collarbone last week. That doctor . . . "

"I know what he said." Vi holds up both hands, her fingers waggling into quotation marks. "'Post-transplant steroid use can lead to osteoporosis.' I'm fine. Don't fuss so much, Ari." Vi is dressed before Ariana can move, her feet quiet on the hardwood. "I'll go feed the ducks."

"Wear your hat!" Ariana flings the hat toward the stairs. "Remember what he said about skin cancer!" Vi's whistling echoes up the stairwell. Ariana frowns and runs downstairs, grabbing the hat en route from the top riser, drops it on the kitchen counter near Vi's favourite stool. She can't wait on Vi, needs to start the duck pâté and confit. Making them brings back memories of Grandmère at the butcher block, her deep laugh, but memories are no comfort when she considers the possibility of life without Vi as well.

During a lull at lunchtime, Ariana steps out of the sweltering kitchen. It's just as hot outside, the air hanging in wavering lines, and sweat leaves a long smear across her sleeve as she wipes her face. She's glad to see light glinting from the windshield of Gordon's truck at the far end of the parking lot. The orchardist's presence means Vi will smile more than usual. Yet every time her sister returns from an outing with Gordon, a noose of resentment tightens around Ariana's ribcage. What kind of woman resents her own sister's friendships? Especially a sister who's bedevilled by physical frailties? Five years since Grandmère summoned Ari home from France, where she was working at her cousin's bakery in Toulouse. It was autumn in the south of France. Ariana returned to a blizzard in Saskatoon, and to Vi, red-faced, hooked up to a dialysis machine, shrilly haranguing the nurses. Soon after, while Grandmère waited in the family room, Violetta and Ariana were rolled into the brightly lit operating room on parallel gurneys, holding hands.

Ariana herself has no time or inclination to socialize. All she's ever wanted is to cook, to own a restaurant. At the end of each day, she has no energy left to spend on a friend, or a lover, for that matter: Vi takes all her emotional currency.

She has read somewhere that saving a life ties two people, in this life and into the next. Not that she's a Buddhist, or even clear on the concepts of reincarnation or karma, but from the moment she offered her kidney to Vi, the feeling intensifying after the surgery itself, she has felt accountable for her older sister. What adds a worrisome chafe to the yoke is the hard fact that organ recipients rarely live more than fifteen years after their transplant. Vi is thirty-five, nowhere near as strong as she used to be when the three of them, Vi, Grandmère and Ariana, spent their time and energies tending the market garden and greenhouses.

Her older sister hasn't sounded so cheerful since her time at university. Before the transplant. Gordon is good for her, no doubt about it. She should simply rejoice that Vi has lost her pinched look.

The lot is jammed with cars. It won't be many weeks before the patio is empty at lunch — the sun is noticeably cooler now that September has fluttered halfway through its rounds. The back door slides soundlessly shut behind her, and Ariana goes back to work, assembling salads, plating galettes, arranging trays of bread and pastries. Violetta strides back and forth through the patio door, her hands full on every pass. It's Ellen's day off, and Ariana, expecting a slow day, had only scheduled Gwen. Vi, who rarely serves, volunteered to wait tables when the parking lot started to fill.

Ariana sighs, catching a glimpse of Vi smiling at a small girl in a gingham sundress. It's just the two of them since Grandmère died, three years gone last April. She misses Grandmère's pragmatic nods and quick hugs. The fact is they won't get rich running a seasonal lakeside bistro and patisserie. It's fine for her, but what does Violetta want to do with the rest of her life? Vi never mentions it, but Ariana feels her sister's clock ticking.

Ariana jumps at an unexpected touch on her shoulder, and a voice in her ear. "I've brought you a few more sour cherry trees."

"Gordon! You startled me."

His short blond hair is dark with sweat, his Smithbilt in his hands. "Sorry, shortcut through the kitchen. D'you mind?"

"No, of course not!" Gordon's freckled face, sunburned despite the hat, reminds her of a puppy, all bounce and wide-mouthed grin. She had been prepared to dislike him the first day he showed up for lunch, another redneck farmer, but his intake of breath and widened eyes at his first taste of her duck galette had disarmed her.

"I set the trees by the back door. They're the hardy varieties I took Vi to see last week at the university. Didn't she tell you? I'll dig them in after lunch."

Ariana recalls her sister returning that day, her hair loose on her shoulders, her face relaxed. Her small, secret smile as Gordon's truck pulled out of the yard.

"Too funny," Ariana says. "The trees' varieties, I mean. Romeo and Juliet."

Gordon flushes right up to his hairline. "Yeah. I guess."

"You're so good to us! Thanks, Gordon."

"No worries. You both work way too hard. Need some lookin' after." He puts on his cowboy hat and light-foots through the screen door toward the patio. Ariana stares at the door as it swings back and forth. Why was he blushing? This man's generosity is wearing down that worry-stone's hard edges.

As if on cue, Ariana hears her sister's voice, a sharp rise of consonants. "*Merde!*"

Spinning around, she sees Vi stumble, caught on the fly by Gordon, his short, stocky body surprisingly nimble as he leaps from three strides away to Vi's side. He stabilizes the plates in her long hands, jokes with the guests who dodge the flying cutlery, ruffles the gingham girl's hair. After all is returned to rights, plates safely delivered, Vi and Gordon stand together beside the Amur maples that line the patio, Gordon's arm folded like a wing over Vi's shoulders, red leaves like bloodstains collecting beside her collar.

Violetta is flushed, patting her chest when she returns to the kitchen. Ariana can feel her own blood pressure climb several points.

"Vi! Are you all right?"

"Just a little light-headed." Vi stoops to rub her calf. "I barked my shin on one of those tomato planters. Did you see that tiny girl, Ari? So cute. She reminded me of you when you were little. Same button nose. I was afraid I'd fall on top of her."

"Sit down, will you? They'll be all right out there without you for a few minutes." Ariana shoves the stool toward her sister. "I'm so terrified every time you take a tumble." She wants to pat her, but Vi has collected so many bruises lately, she's reluctant to pat anywhere. Nothing broken. A relief. But the injuries seem to be coming more rapidly. It's as if her sister's inner spring is unwinding.

She settles for a quick hug but misjudges its placement. Vi winces and leans away. "Oh, Vi, I'm sorry. That's it, this is the last time you talk me into letting you wait tables." To Ariana's surprise, Vi doesn't put up an argument. "You're lucky Gordon was there. He brought more trees."

"He said as much."

"Here. Eat something."

Vi plucks the slice of bread from Ariana's hand, pecks at it, swallows.

"Vi! Stay put a minute longer!" Her sister's grin is back on her face before she disappears through the swinging door.

Gordon has been here almost every day this month. On each trip, he has unloaded something unexpected from the back of the pickup — shrubs, rosebushes, and once, a new hoe to replace Ariana's after it had snapped in her hands. Ariana has offered him money, but he shrugs her off, his chuckle reminding her of the coots' clattering voices in the reed beds. "Maybe lunch later?" he always responds, rubbing his chin and grinning before he slides away. "I'll just go see if I can help Vi. She in the office?"

Ariana rolls pastry as she looks out the kitchen window, the dough pooling beneath her rolling pin the way the water ripples around the teals and pintails. Bistro Étoile is a deliberate re-creation of the small lakeside cafés she visited in France, right down to the two-tone umbrellas fluttering over the patio tables. Grandmère had immediately seen the possibilities of the idea when Ariana broached it after her return from France. "You've learned all I can teach you," she said. "It's time." Her square hands, so like Ariana's, shook slightly as she handed Ariana a cheque. The morning they opened four years ago, Ariana stood outside beside her, their shoulders just touching, watching the umbrellas. Waiting. When the first cars edged down the long driveway beside the lake, she hugged Grandmère and went inside to cook, a tiny prayer to St. Honoré, the patron saint of pastry chefs, flitting in her head. *Please, make it last, make this last. Keep my sister safe.* She didn't dare say it out loud.

The dough beneath her hands feels springy. Ariana fits it into a tart pan, her fingertips fluting the edge into a wave. Vi's near-accident this afternoon is a wake-up.

Ariana flicks the switch on the overhead fan. Through its muffled roar, she hears Vi's voice.

"Are there any cookies left? What about profiteroles?" Vi, standing before the counter, holds out a basket, her grey eyes wide, smiling. "That man has the most amazing appetite!" She reaches out and tucks a strand of Ariana's cropped black hair back behind her ear. She's humming under her breath, a French nursery tune that Ariana vaguely recognizes. Vi always hums when Gordon's in the vicinity. Her face changes then, from its normal narrow aspect, somehow becoming rounder, more childlike.

Ariana finds herself humming along. She fills the basket with cookies, then gives Vi a little shove. "Go on then." She nods, observing the two of them bending over the tomato planters. Gordon is Vi's first real friend since the transplant. On his first visit, after appreciatively downing the galette, Gordon consumed several pastries, two double espressos, plum eau de vie, candied hazelnuts. He stayed long after the patio emptied, gazing at the lake as it swelled into wavelets under the heavy westerly breeze. At four o'clock, he braved Ariana's kitchen. "Excuse me?"

Ariana looked up from her corner desk. Up close, she saw that his fair hair was muddled with grey and two vertical lines cut deep clefts in his forehead. His hands on his cowboy hat were weathered but clean.

"Can I help you? Your bill, maybe? My sister will be — " Violetta was upstairs, rebalancing her blood sugars with a shot of insulin and a bowl of lentil soup.

"Oh, no! I don't need anything else," he said. "You must be the chef-sister. I just wanted to say thanks, to you, and to my lovely server. Amazing." Violetta glided down the stairs at that moment, and Gordon's steady gaze left Ariana's face for hers. "Everything. Just . . . amazing."

The garden looks nearly done, plants slumping from last night's frost, when Ariana carries her basket out to harvest the last of the zucchini. She's ready to rest, too. While she usually appreciates the constancy of their clientele, today she wishes they'd all just pack their bags and fly south, like the grebes and geese. The winter closure lets her recover from early mornings and long hours on her feet in the kitchen. Lets new recipe ideas bubble to the surface. Beyond the raspberries, she spots the new cherry trees, slim whips in a cluster, already planted.

Vi looks exhausted, leaning on the kitchen counter, when Ariana returns with the vegetables.

"Sit down, Vi." Ariana drags over a stool. "Has Gordon left? I wanted to say thank you."

"You just missed him," Vi says. "Stop fussing!" But she obediently perches on the stool. "I've been thinking, it's been years since you had went out and had some fun. When did you last have a date, Ari?"

"Not interested," Ariana replies shortly. "I've got plenty to keep me busy here."

"I know you do. Just asking. You could use a break." Her voice changes tone slightly, dropping. "That guy you met in Toulouse — ever hear anything from him?"

"No."

"All right. You don't have to snap at me."

"Sorry. I didn't mean to. My hands are full, Vi."

Vi hangs her head. "I know it's on my account," she says, flushing as she makes eye contact with Ariana. "But Gordon and I have been talking, Ariana."

"Yes, I know. I saw the trees, he's already planted them, at the south end of the raspberry canes. Fast worker, that man."

Vi smirks. "He thinks we should build a berm. Plant more trees, a whole orchard. More berries. Turn the place into a real agri-tourism gate-to-plate destination. And make wines." She gathers up the zucchini and heads for the sink without looking directly at her sister.

"What are you suggesting? We aren't wine makers, and neither of us has the energy or time to take on another project. It'd take years to learn how to make fruit wine."

"Gordon is. A wine maker, I mean." Vi's pale cheeks darken. "I've invited him to come back tonight. For an after-hours dinner." She looks sideways at Ariana. "I want you there. At the table, I mean, with us, not in the kitchen."

"What? Why's that? You never invite people to dinner."

"We want to talk to you. About . . . about the future. So let's just eat what Grandmère would serve, right? Something simple, whatever you've already made. Bread, duck, beans. Don't fuss. Please."

"What do you mean, the future? Whose future?" Ariana, mystified, standing flatfooted in the kitchen. Vi, smiling to herself, tidying the dining room.

The women set the best patio table, but the wind blows in off the lake with a vengeance. It begins to rain, slanting drops that cut through the air and the lake's surface. Autumn has arrived, abruptly, as it always does.

"We'll have to eat indoors, Vi. Sorry."

Violetta carries in the sunflowers, scatters their petals on the tablecloth, adds glassware, cutlery, candles. When the table is set, she restlessly washes and re-washes glasses, polishes immaculate forks. Ariana retreats to the kitchen and turns on the radio. When she lifts the lids of the pots, the aroma of anise-scented duck underlaid by earthy beans fills the room. Vi comes in, prowling the narrow walkway, picks up baking sheets and rolling pins, sets them down with a clatter and bang.

Ariana nudges her. "For crying out loud, Vi. Go for a little walk, the rain's stopped! I'll call you." She leans against the stove, watches the vast sky streaked with clouds. On the lake, the wild waterbirds are gathering, canvasbacks, buffleheads, teals, merganzers in matched pairs. They lift off in successive waves, heading south, their wings drumming, water slapping.

Vi returns, slightly out of breath. When she stumbles over the lip of the kitchen door, Ariana leaps, trembling, her arms open, remembering as she scrambles the graceful arc of Gordon's rescue. Before Ariana can cross the kitchen, Vi regains her balance. Ariana feels a heavy knot beneath her sternum. She can't guarantee their lives or their income, can't keep Vi safe, can't even catch her when she trips.

"I'm all right." Vi opens the cooler and pulls out a bottle, splashes wine into two glasses and sits on her favourite stool, her miscreant feet tucked under her. "The hospital isn't our only anniversary, remember? Our fourth season, nearly done." She hands her a glass. "*Salut.*"

"*Salut.*"

They sit at the counter in silence.

Ariana hears the roar of a defective muffler. Gordon's truck. The creases in Vi's forehead ease as he hurries in and lightly kisses her tidy braid of hair. Observing that intimate gesture, Ariana wonders what else she hasn't taken note of.

"Sorry I'm late," he says. "Did you tell her, Vi?"

Vi's face turns pink. "I was waiting for you." She grabs Gordon's hand. "We want to have a baby, Ariana."

"What?" The glass in Ariana's hand almost slips through her fingers. Wine spills on her lap. Gordon, stifling a grin, picks up a towel and passes it to her. Ariana's hands flutter. "You've never said anything about babies before!" Only once before — a wistful comment made a couple years ago, watching two toddlers with stains around their mouths follow their mother from stall to stall at the market, their chubby hands clutching half-eaten strawberries. Ariana had dismissed it as a passing fancy, far too risky for a diabetic with only one kidney and a short life expectancy. "Gordon? He's like a brother! Isn't he? Aren't you?" She looks from one to the other.

Vi starts to laugh. "A brother? That's what you thought I felt? Oh, Ariana. You need to get out more."

Ariana flushes and ducks her head. "You could have told me," she mutters. "Why didn't you?" Her sternum contracts and releases. Gordon, his arm around Vi beside the maple trees.

Catching her, his arms briefly suspending her above the earth. Blushing in the kitchen.

"You said it yourself, you have enough to worry about, Ari."

"But a baby!" Ariana looks at Gordon. "This feels awfully out of the blue."

"Sorry, Ariana," Gordon says, reaches for the wine bottle. "Can I?" She nods, and he refills their glasses, then pours a third. "We've been talking about it for awhile, but didn't want to bring it up until we'd worked out the details. We've got it all figured out, and we want your . . . your blessing, I suppose. Your good will. I don't want Vi to wait tables anymore."

"I'm with you there."

"I thought I'd build an addition onto the house, an east wing, so we wouldn't intrude on you. Then a winery on the north side. I'll put in more canes, they'll be producing in two years. And more cherry trees. Maybe haskap, they're doing well in field trials, and more rhubarb. Surprising, what good wine rhubarb makes."

"Grandmère made rhubarb wine," Vi interjects, her eyes bright. "Remember, Ariana? No, maybe not, you were too young."

"Never mind the wine! What about you?"

The sun breaks through the patchwork clouds, long shadows, surreal light.

"What about me?" Vi touches her sister's arm, gently, like leaves descending. "I love Gordon. This is more of a chance at life than I thought I'd have. It's just like the birds, Ari. Things come and go in their own time."

"I know. But that doesn't mean I want to think about . . . you dying."

"Then don't. But I want you to be to my baby what Grandmère was to you. When it's time."

"I don't understand."

"You wanted to talk about what next, Ari. Well, what next has arrived, and it's time to talk about it. No, don't fuss. It's a fact. All this day-to-day stuff is just detail. We have to talk about the big picture. About what might happen. I'll need your help. With the baby, I mean."

"But, Vi — "

The lines in Vi's face loosen. "Ariana, you know what's coming. So does Gordon. I may have ten years."

Ariana shivers. Her innards clench and release, freeing a blur of relief and guilt and chagrin. She knows exactly what Vi intends to say.

"If we do have a child, and if . . . when . . . well, I want you to help Gordon raise it."

Vi's voice trails off.

Ariana looks at Gordon, his hands sheltering Vi's, and understanding flickers, like light on the water. "But I'm not mother material."

"Don't be ridiculous. What do you think you've been doing for the past four years, caring for me?"

"That doesn't make me a mother!"

"You're right. Sorry." Violetta reaches out, her hand nesting on Ariana's skin. "I'm not going anywhere anytime soon. We can learn together."

"And the restaurant?"

"Listen, Ari, I don't know all the answers or what will happen. I don't. But I'm willing to take it on trust if you are. It'll all work out. Always does." She looks curiously at Ari. Winks, her sightless eye a moon in the fading evening light. "You're over-thinking this. What does your gut tell you?"

"My gut?" Ariana breathes in. "I don't . . . "

"Do you need some time to think about it?"

"No, Vi. I don't need to think about it."

The lake is still, the autumn moon re-emerging as the rain slows. Ariana slings a jacket over her shoulders and leaves Vi and Gordon together in the kitchen. She can see the shadows of their figures move close together as the patio's outdoor lights flicker on. Something close to envy fills her as she watches them dance.

Wandering along the path beside the lakeshore, tears on Ariana's cheeks feel cool in the breeze as she tries to imagine Vi's crooked smile superimposed on a child's face. She pulls her hands from their pockets. Wide palms. Square knuckles. A maker's hands. So like Grandmère's. Ahead of her, several coots stop squabbling and lift clumsily into the air with a heavy drumming of wings.

The envy fades, replaced by a current of possibilities. She wipes her cheeks with her jacket sleeve and stoops, picking up a smooth small stone that just fits within the cradle of her palm. A rapid release, and it skips across the lake, one two three four five skimming arcs that the avocets ignore. With a bobbing nod of her head, Ariana enumerates each quick touch of stone to water. She lifts her face to the birds, their impermeable bodies graceful in the air, their beaks pointing south. Their parabolic lives will bring them back in the spring. That much is a certainty.

The Quinzhee

HE WAS FOURTEEN THE YEAR WE built the quinzhee, and I was seventeen, the youngest kid in grade twelve. *Old enough to know better,* our taciturn Irish mother was in the habit of saying. She never said it to me again after he died, but I have said it to myself often enough.

I have trained myself to never utter those words to my own son or daughter. But they reverberate in my head as I watch my twins go out into the sunlight, intent on testing themselves against the world. That is ridiculous, I know. All of life involves risk, and they could shatter their fragile bodies by sheer happenstance on the sidewalk right in front of this house. I am a cautious mother, in a way I never thought possible when I was seventeen and invulnerable, and Leo grows impatient with me even though he understands. "You have to let them go, Jess," he says. But today, on the first anniversary of my mother's death, it is too late to beg her forgiveness, or Jeremy's, and I cannot find an olive branch within me to extend to my own hand.

We lived south of Calgary, in the foothills near Priddis. God's country, my Alberta-born father liked to say. On early spring mornings, riding my horse through the aspens, when the light lit the far flanks of the Rockies, I knew he was right.

Jeremy was bouncing in his seat on the school bus one afternoon. "A quinzhee's the coolest thing, Jess. You heap up all this snow and then you hollow it out into a dome. I want us to build one. It won't take very long, and it'll be fun."

"Jere, it's freakin' cold out there." It was minus thirty-two that February day, and had been for a week.

Leo was in the seat behind us. He pulled his toque over his curls and shook his head at my brother as he made his way up the aisle. "My stop. Man, are you crazy? See you tomorrow, Jess. Call me if you need help with your Chaucer. I think I have it figured."

I nodded gratefully, then let myself be persuaded by my brother. Anything sounded more appealing that afternoon than reading Chaucer. I didn't understand him at all, kept skipping ahead to the Romantic poets, Byron, and Shelley's skylarks. I wanted to write odes to birds too, and kept a journal of all the birds I saw. On our morning walks to the bus, the chickadees and nuthatches hung in a cloud above our heads, eager for the peanuts I carried in my pockets. They'd swoop down, falling like a piece of heaven onto my palm if I stood quietly and held out a handful. I had wings of paper describing them and other birds jammed in every pocket of every jacket I owned.

Mom always wanted to know what we were up to, and her County Cork accent got thick when she thought we were heading for trouble or when she decided Leo had been in my room for too long. But we managed to duck out of the house unnoticed. Jeremy detoured to the barn and came back with grain shovels over his shoulder, Mario, our giant black schnauzer, plunging ahead. Cold settled on my cheeks and forehead, numbness that I impatiently smothered with my scarf. Jeremy led me to a clearing, a stone's throw from where the lane's double track curved toward the house, on the edge of the south pasture, aspens lining the north edge as a windbreak. It was a strategic spot: close enough to the house to meet Mom's approval, but out of her actual sight. The snow lay untouched except for the deer tracks to the edge of the dugout, and the kiss of a pheasant wing alongside the imprint of a claw.

"Here! This is perfect!" He showed me where to heap the snow, and we shoveled until well past sunset, sweat collecting along our backs and ribcages under our parkas and thermal underwear. I cut snow in perfect blocks that seemed to be made of nothing but light. Each block shattered when I dropped it from my shovel onto the growing pile, its mass reduced to crumbs of nothing.

"Jere, it's gonna take us forever. This stuff doesn't look like it will ever be solid."

"Come on, Jess, just a bit more." Jeremy looked frail, but he had been shoveling grain since he was a grasshopper, his skinny arms toughened into wire. I bent and carried, cut and dumped, finally throwing down my shovel and collapsing into a drift of untouched whiteness.

"I quit." I stretched my arms, then moved my legs. "Help me up, Jere, I'm stuck." After he pried me loose, I turned and looked. A perfect snow angel. The adjacent snow pile was close to four feet tall. Astounded, I paced off its perimeter. "Thirty-four steps! Wow, Jeremy! Is that big enough?"

My brother smiled smugly. "Nearly twelve feet in diameter, Jess. We're halfway there."

A shadow fell across the slanted incline of snow, Dad tracking us down. "You kids! Haven't you heard your mother calling you for supper?" His voice was as sharp as the wind that caught my face full on. I was immediately aware that the sweat on my skin was cooling, and snow was wadded under my jacket.

Jeremy walked beside Dad, talking with his hands as he explained our efforts, and I entered the kitchen alone to get both barrels from Mom. She slammed an empty pan onto the counter and crashed the oven door shut before she turned to me. Her black hair was pushed untidily behind her ears, and the lines around her blue eyes were stretched as tight as her voice.

"Where have you been? Where's your brother? Jeremy! Get in here! It's nearly minus forty! I've been worried sick. Jesus Mary, Jess, what were you thinking at all? You're old enough to know better."

"Sorry, Mom. I lost track of time." I shrugged and headed upstairs to wash, Jeremy close behind me.

All that week after school, while I cradled the phone and listened to Leo read his idea of what Chaucer should sound like, Jeremy went out to the snow pile with a shovel, then pored over a heap of library books, anything with something to say about quinzhees. At supper, he recounted his findings. "Listen! This is so cool!" he said, practically levitating off his chair. "Every quinzhee has to sinter." He launched into a complicated explanation of powder solidifying by heat, then sidetracked, taking a wild guess at the height of the growing snowpile. Our dad, the former bank manager turned rancher, observed Jeremy's enthusiasm with approval, and demanded that he calculate the volume and weight of snow shoveled. Jeremy, his hair still damp from sweat and exertion, struggled with the formulas, counted on his fingers, then forgot the task in favour of expounding on the origins of quinzhees among the Dog-Ribs and Cree up north along the Canadian Shield. "And the Métis trappers too, so they could stay out overnight on their traplines. Hey Dad, we could set up traplines!"

"Mister research king, how about you spend less time on quinzhees and more time on your homework?" Mom laughed, but she didn't sound amused. She was leery of Jeremy's propensity for research, stung by his announcement one day that her Celtic name meant 'sorrowful'. "She died of a broken heart, Mom. How cool is that?"

"Not cool at all," Mom had snapped. "Tragic. She leaned out of a chariot to smash her head on a rock."

This time Dad intervened. "It's okay, Deirdre. He's learning lots. But no traplines, laddie." He reminded Jeremy that he would have to kill, gut and skin the animals, and Jeremy quickly lost interest. But his fascination with the quinzhee didn't wane.

Days later, the snow pile stood seven feet high and we began to hollow out a shell. Even Chaucer seemed more appealing, and I felt the ticking clock of approaching midterm exams. But Jeremy was possessed, his quinzhee demon urging us both to hours in the cold. We carved an entrance like a keyhole into the south face where the wind was at its least fractious. Then Jeremy used the grain shovel, kneeling to scrape a tunnel into the core of the pile. I was relegated to clearing the entrance, snow flying between my knees as I struggled to keep up.

"I built a platform, up off the ground. Come look." Jeremy said from inside the quinzhee. I could barely hear his voice unless I knelt at the keyhole and put my head into the tunnel. I inched inside on my belly and elbows. Jeremy, knees up to his cheeks, perched on a small escarpment. "Stop!"

I froze. He pointed at the curved ceiling. Patches of light played like seawater, washed blue and pale green, through the packed snow.

"Look at that. So beautiful," he breathed. "Let's see how thick the snow is." He made me wiggle out to pull a twig from the nearby aspen. I passed the stick in to him, a good foot long, and he jammed it into the ceiling's luminous arc. When the twig's entire length was buried, he waved me out of the tunnel. Outside, no twig was visible on the snow's curving wall.

We recounted the latest development at dinner. Our mother raised her eyes to meet my father's, and she said quietly, "You'll not be going in there alone, Jeremy."

My father came into my bedroom later and made urgent "get off the phone now" motions at me. After I said goodnight to Leo, he sat down along the edge of my bed, pushing my phone and my copy of Shelley aside. "Jessie, you remember your mom talking about your uncle Brett? I know she hardly ever mentions him. Before we were married, on the farm in the Peace Country, Brett suffocated in a granary full of barley."

"Dad, that's ancient history."

"It might be to you, but your mom still misses her brother." He gathered me into a hug.

My face was muffled against his sweater. "I know this story. It's awful. Why are you talking about this now, Dad?"

"You know your mother. She thinks that Brett might have survived if your uncle Peter had been around. Peter was driving the grain truck. It was harvest, and they were rushing to combine the last quarter. Brett lost his balance and fell into the granary. Your mother is superstitious, you know that, and nervous about this snow fort. Don't you leave Jeremy alone out there, you hear?"

"Dad! Why did she send you to do her dirty work? She always does that. She makes you take her bad news to people."

"Don't cry, Sugarplum. Your mom didn't mean any harm. She just had a bad feeling. You know, that goose."

My mother. A goose walking over her grave. It wasn't her own grave she was haunted by. It was everyone else's. I swore I would never be such a worrier. Never. But to my father, I just nodded. "Okay, Dad. Whatever."

By the following week, the quinzhee was a glittering room with a curved inner ceiling, like the onion dome on the Ukrainian church we had seen on a school trip to Calgary.

Leo came over to look, and admired the quinzhee's even dimensions, but Mom wouldn't come near it. Mario liked to lie outside the entrance, whining and snuffling when we both disappeared inside. We took turns as inside ferret and outside snow scraper. The ferret used the old short-handled hoe, holding it horizontally to scrape the walls, kicking the snow down to ground level. The scraper scuffed the loose snow away from the entrance. When we described this to our parents, even our mother laughed. She said it reminded her of that Steve McQueen movie, *The Great Escape*, when the Tunnel King's sidekicks scuffed dirt from inside their pant legs onto the ground right under the noses of the German guards. I had seen the movie on TV at Leo's not long before, so the story and characters was fresh in my mind, and I explained it to Jeremy. At breakfast, I called him "Danny," after Charles Bronson, the claustrophobic Polish tunneler in the movie who panics when the ceiling caves in, and my mother winced, her smile fading. I didn't call him Danny again.

Jeremy cajoled me into going out when the moon was high and we gathered candles to illuminate the quinzhee. Mom handed us the matches reluctantly.

"I'm not liking this affair at all."

"Mom, I've called Leo, he's coming over, so don't worry. And Dad said — "

"Don't you be quoting your father at me, my girl. You're old enough — "

"I know, I know!"

The quinzhee's platform was just big enough for the three of us to lie side by side, reggae music flooding from Leo's Walkman. Jeremy loved the ceiling. He said it reminded him of a caliph's tented canopy, studded with diamonds and embroidered in silver. I just laughed and threw snow at him. I was going to be the poet, not him. He and Leo were both going to be scientists and count all the stars that hadn't been found yet. We learned that the easiest way to leave the quinzhee was like otters, head first, sliding down on our bellies from the platform and emerging from the tunnel shaking with laughter.

One evening, it started to snow as if heaven had opened its vault. After supper, we pulled on our snow wear, and stepped into the gale, but couldn't see our path to the quinzhee. We crept through the yard by memory, hands out like blind beggars. The aspens north of the dugout whispered and whistled.

"Jeremy, it's too dark," I said. "Let's go back, C'mon. This is no fun, I'm freezing." I couldn't see his face, but his hand was reassuringly there in mine. We turned our shoulders to the wind and retreated.

When we came home from school the next day, the bus wobbled on the grid road, sliding and skidding so ominously that even Leo and the other seniors who sat in the last four rows were silenced until Mr. Wiebe headed the wheels solidly south. As we walked past the clearing, Jeremy grabbed my arm. I could barely hear his voice through the layers of scarf over his mouth. "Let's go to the quinzhee right now. It'll be so quiet. We can listen to the birds. Maybe you can write a new poem."

"No, let's go have something to eat first, Jere. The birds are all hiding in the trees. We won't hear anything."

"You jam tart. I'm goin'."

He was so stubborn. He shouldered his backpack and marched toward the dugout. The snow fluttered and swirled in eddies at his back. I hesitated. Mom would have a fit. But I was hungry, and I would come right back with a thermos of tea. I headed down the driveway.

The house was empty except for Mario, asleep beside the stove. He woke when he heard me, yawning and stretching, and snuffled my face when I bent to say hi. I put on the kettle and picked up the note from where it lay on the table beside a plate stacked high with raisin cookies. Dad's tidy script, a relic from his business days, said they were both gone to town on errands, and please put the lasagna in the oven by four thirty. Mario thumped his stubby tail on the floor as I fed him a cookie, and he curled up at my feet. I poured the boiling water into the teapot, and picked up my book.

When I looked up from Shelley, my tea was tepid and the kitchen was growing dark. A sharp blast of wind rattled the windows. Mario barked once, sharply. I could feel the house shiver and shake.

I poured the tea into a thermos and scrambled into my parka. Anxiety caught in my throat. I lurched out the door, Mario jostling for space on the stoop. "Chill, big guy. Let's go get Jeremy. He'll be ready for some tea."

Mario whined when I led the way toward the dugout. He threaded his tall body between my legs and I stumbled, dropping the thermos. I let it go. The wind yanked my hood from my forehead. Mario came to heel, and I leaned on his shoulder as we pushed against the gale, snow like grit in my eyes and face. I turned around and pulled my scarf up over my nose, wanting to be eight again, wishing Mom was here to tighten and snug its folds, wanting Dad's arm to hang onto. Jeremy would be worrying, or trying to find his way back. I had to get to him.

I didn't recognize the quinzhee when I stumbled into its curved wall.

An aspen had fallen, the wind carrying it like a twig across the north side of the quinzhee, the rest of the structure collapsed into a heap without discernible edges.

"Jeremy! Jeremy!"

Beside me, Mario started to howl.

I was crying, gulps that I choked on and couldn't swallow, as I dug frantically at the entry with my hands, afraid to leave for a shovel, afraid of what I might hear or see, desperate for my brother to be whole and breathing, calling his name over and over. Mario kept trying to lick my face. I couldn't push him away, and as I dug in the dark and the wind, his tongue and my tears glazed my face in a sheer ice cake that cracked with each sob. I wanted to hear Jeremy's voice telling me again about the blue and green sparkles that lit the quinzhee's ceiling. I wished I had never helped hollow its heart, and I wished my parents were home.

It was half an hour before the truck finally rolled silently down the lane, its headlights around the curve slicing through the falling snow to illuminate me where I knelt. I stayed where I was, scraping snow from the pile, my head gone numb and hopeless. My tears had stopped, and I was shivering, wheezing with fear and cold.

My mother, screaming like the banshees, had leaped from the pickup before it came to a stop. She ran across the field and fell to her knees beside me, clawing with her gloved hands at the jammed entrance. My father, right behind her, stopped, stared at me where I knelt at the ruined walls, then came to my mother's side. He pulled her away with gentle hands, and carried her back to the truck. When he came back to me in the whirling snow, his face was white slate, his mouth like solid iron. He wrapped his arms around me and we walked around to the front of the truck, out of Mom's earshot.

"Jess."

I could barely hear him. He put his mouth next to my ear. "Jessie! I want you to drive your mother to the house. Call 911. Then call Leo's family. Ask them to bring the John Deere with the front end loader. Stay with your mother. I'll start moving the tree. Can you do that?"

I nodded.

They say that when disaster strikes, time slows and stretches, turns to pulled taffy, and that you can see through its membranes to the other side. That it protects the innocent and the victims from the truth's stark immediacy. I don't know if that is true. I do recall that long trip up the driveway, my mother weeping, her face turned away from me, the truck groaning in low gear as the storm raged, as one endless moment edged in the silk of unfeeling time. It was the last semblance of peace I would feel for decades.

Witnessing my mother's sorrow, the intensity of her loss when her favourite child died so young, so needlessly, and enduring her years of subsequent silence to me, chipped away the pleasure I'd felt in poetry and birds. I didn't want to have children of my own despite Leo's pleas. I put off marrying him for years, struggled in therapy, my mother's grief and anger breaking over me, merging with my guilt.

I became an anthropologist, not a poet. I work alone in my home office, poring over maps and computer screens, researching boys' coming-of-age rites in central Asia. Sparkles from dangling glass spinners in the window flame the wall, amber and ultra-violet, scarlet and aquamarine. But whenever I close my eyes, the light refracts, translucent as the quinzhee's roof, Jeremy's shroud of snow.

I finally married Leo at thirty-two, a year after my father died. Each night, I wrapped his arms around me like a blanket. "Hold me tight, Leo." He is the only one, other than Jeremy, who lay beneath the ceiling of the quinzhee with me, and he knows how the sky spins and wheels.

The night after we learned that we were going to have twins, I lay beside him, unmoving. "Will she rejoice or curse?"

"Who, sweetie?"

"Mom. Who else?"

When we went to see her, she did neither. She looked at me bleakly. "I wish you joy of them."

We named them Jeremy and Deirdre. For the sorrows.

Appetites

THE BLUE JAY IS HANGING AROUND again. I haven't seen him for months, and now here he is in the front yard, shrieking as he clings to the twigs on the outside of the birdfeeder, his crest catching on its roof as he pokes his spiky beak inside to get at the platform. Finally he gives up, flies the few feet to the ground. Pecks at the peanuts that lie scattered among the sunflower seeds in the meagre grass at the foot of the cherry tree.

There were years when I couldn't abide the smell of peanuts, years I wondered if I'd ever go back to eating them, if I'd ever make peanut and chocolate tart for the dessert menu or peanut butter and honey sandwiches for my kid's school lunch. Course, that was before the big allergy lookout — peanuts are *verboten* now at Jared's school. But it's not the peanuts I want. It's my appetite. The enthusiasm that blue jay brought to his precarious roost on the edge of the feeder. The alacrity that sent him scuttling through the grass to eat. That's what I miss on these colourless days. That, and my sense of taste. Everything I put into my mouth tastes like scorched beans or burnt nuts. My nose recognizes just a few aromas, the most pungent ones — garlic, sweat, caramelized sugar that's gone past amber to the edge of bitterness.

My MD was sanguine. "A small anomaly, maybe stress," she told me three months ago as I perched on the edge of the examining table in her spartan office. Easy for her to say, to suspect that the flu and a nasal infection had simultaneously fried my sensory input channel. As if I'm a damn computer or a video game. That I'll regain my palate. Eventually. That's no consolation. I'm a cook. My life revolves around having a highly developed sense of taste, a nose that can tell the difference between caramelized and burnt. What if it doesn't come back? I cook from memory now. I haven't told my boss.

Lance comes into the kitchen at work as I dust a steaming pot of clam and leek chowder with smoked paprika.

"Hi, Chef," I say.

He nods absently, heading for his paperwork. "Sandy's replacement starts today. Guy named Maurice, friend of Philip's."

I think of leprechauns when the new waiter follows Philip into the kitchen. There's no Irish accent, but he's spry and merry, soft voice and bright eyes, his nose and cheeks too puckish to be considered handsome. When lunch service ends, I pull out the box grater and start on the beets while I ask him where he's from.

"I've lived in lots of places," Maurice says. Is he trying to be coy? Shy? He doesn't seem shy.

"He's been to Europe six times. Worked on a cruise line in the Mediterranean, he's just the most terrible flirt," Philip interjects as he unloads dishes at the dish pit. A wine glass falls and shatters at Maurice's feet. "Damn! Sweep that up, will ya?" Maurice folds himself forward, one hand on the broom, watching me and not the glass shards in the dustpan.

I'm ladling the chowder into containers for the walk-in when Lance walks past. He backtracks, picks up a clean spoon. Dips it into the pot and tastes. Makes a face. The spoon clatters into the sink.

"Flat, Stacy." I wince as he adds a handful of kosher salt and squeezes a lemon into the pot. He tastes the soup again, his long horse cheeks flat and incurious. "Another bad day?"

"Yeah." When I look at the clock, my heart lurches. So much yet to get done. "Gotta go early, Chef, Jared has a basketball game."

But I can't distract him. "You know, yesterday's lentil salad was salty. And so was last week's sweet potato soufflé. S'up?"

I shrug. Let him think I'm tired or preoccupied. Working in a small restaurant will give anyone wrinkles. The long hours make me tear out my hair, and I can't count how many of Jared's games I've missed. Whatever let me think I could do this alone?

A couple hours later, when I step outside to the bus stop, winter is in every breath of wind. A battered grey Corvette pulls up, starfishing cracks in every window, Maurice at the wheel. "Give you a ride?"

"I'm going to the north side," I say. He nods and I climb in. "How was your first shift?"

"Oh fine, you know, same old."

"Up here." I wave at the boulevard. Maurice swings his car around the corner as if he was parking a yacht. Ten minutes pass in silence before I catch sight of Jared, hurtling toward us through the school's gate, ambushing the car door to lean through the window.

"Hey, Mom! Cool car! Can I go for a ride?"

"Honey, we've got to get home. Maybe Maurice can take you for a spin another day. Thanks, Maurice, see you at work."

"Hang on half a sec," Maurice says. "I may as well run you home, I've come this far." The growling car makes short work of the trip. Jared, fiddling with the power windows, is all smiles when Maurice promises another ride. "Next time, bud. See ya, Stacy."

Today's special is rogan josh, my favourite lamb curry, rich with garam masala and ginger. I've made it dozens of times. It's typical of what I most love about cooking, that transformation as raw ingredients soften and blend with each other, their edges melting into something new, opening, like lovers tangled in a bed. I know, and to the milligram, exactly how much lemon juice those hot peppers need as flame tamers, how much salt reins in the sharp edge of the spices, when I mix in the yoghurt. Before lunch service, Lance's spoon dips, pauses. He nods. Why doesn't he comment on it? Why just mention the dishes that need help?

Seems I'm messing up everything. After twelve years of marriage, Matthew left me. No hint he was unhappy. He just left one evening after dinner. He still loved me, he said, but he needed to be himself. I've never hindered you, I said, why can't you be yourself with us? What about Jared? Mushrooms on linguini. I can't imagine the smell of mushrooms and sherry without hearing the door slowly creak and click into silence. Took a suitcase, left everything behind in the apartment for Jared and me. Sleeping alone in our king-size bed after years of sheltering within the curve of Matthew's body, I feel stripped to the bone. Jared still doesn't believe it. Thinks his daddy's coming back every night to tuck him in. I want to believe that too. But the divorce papers changed that when they dropped through the mail slot last fall. If he ever comes home, I'd throw things at him. And then hug him.

Lance is a good boss. He puts up with me without ever getting past so much as a simmer. I've been working the lunch and prep shift here since Jared started school, five years now, a lifetime in the restaurant world, where cooks and chefs come and go like yesterday's menus. Lance tolerates my occasional short-notice absences with good grace when Jared is sick and can't go to school. My kid is too old for day care, too young to leave home alone. Still young enough to fling his arms around me when I come home with the pungency of onions and garlic clinging to my skin

"Taste everything," Lance said when he hired me. I was a good cook then, but green, no experience in a professional kitchen. He looked up at me from his cluttered desk in the corner of the kitchen, his face serious. He's not a laughing kind of guy. "Build benchmarks of flavour and balance, an internal reference library. Write things down and keep mental notes too. Eventually you won't need a cookbook." I've mastered pastry and desserts in the time I've been here at the Blue Heron. That peanut and chocolate tart is our most popular dessert, a real challenge. Its flavours revolve around a burnt orange caramel sauce infused with rosemary. If I can't balance it, if I sprinkle too many salt crystals on top of the chocolate as it sets, all those expensive ingredients, all my effort and time, it's all wasted. You can't undo things. He's taught me how to build nuanced layers of flavour as elegant as a debutante's ball gown. But if my palate doesn't come back, I'm sunk. We change the menu on Tuesdays, so every week begins fresh, a new collection of dishes to try. No map. Just my appetite.

When I get home, the message light on the kitchen desk phone is blinking. Jared. Game cancelled, gone to Omar's for supper and a sleepover, tomorrow is Saturday, Mom, okay? His voice like toffee. I eat mechanically, standing at the fridge door, leftover cold chicken and Shanghai noodles, then lie down for a few minutes on Jared's bed. The reeky boy-scent that clings to his duvet and sheets gets through, and I close my eyes. Just for a minute.

I wake to the shriek of the phone.

"Stacy. You coming in?"

Damn. I slept through the night on my son's bed. My eyes are grit and glass in the slanted sunlight, long angular rays like faded hopes, a wan puddle on the kitchen counter. This time two years ago, Matthew was buying me orchids to keep the dark at bay. My skin smells like yesterday's food. Hate that stale air hanging on my clothes. Matthew always said he didn't mind the odour, but I do. The past, reluctant to let go.

The bus stop is two blocks away, air biting as I wait, long teeth like javelins. Weekday mornings, Jared rides with me to school, one arm around my neck, standing on the floor beside my seat, eye to eye, level grey, like the sea in a storm. "Maybe he'll be back today, Mom." He says the same thing every day. Every morning, I kiss my son and watch him walk up the path into the school. Then I go to work, cooking food that tastes like dust and ashes.

Lance is at the counter when I arrive, a boning knife in his hand. "Sorry, sorry," I say, button my whites and pick up my knives from the toolbox under his desk.

"Yeah yeah. Be gentle with that pastry," he admonishes as I grab my favourite rolling pin. Half an hour later, the pastry is cooling on the rack and the chocolate ganache is setting in a smooth brown pool as I bend close to the counter, sprinkling salt flakes. The caramel is bubbling on the stove behind me, slowly turning amber.

"Stacy! Get on with it!" Lance, at my elbow, shakes his head in frustration. "Get a grip, woman. We have the rest of the ducks to take apart for confit and brunch prep to start."

I turn back to the tart, keep my cringe invisible. Philip, going past with cutlery to polish, brings me a cappo on his next trip. My good friend.

On Monday, as I strain the chicken stock, I tease Maurice, sleek in narrow black shirt and fitted brocade vest. "Snazzy duds. That the Mediterranean influence?"

He grins. "A man learns things in Europe. Ever been to Ireland? The roads are a foot wide, the cars are tiny, it rains, sheep everywhere, everyone drives like they're in a rally. On the wrong side of the road. Like Italians, only crazier. Harrr-der to on-derrr-stand."

I laugh. The chicken carcasses jut out of the sieve, angular as runway models, all bone and tendon, flopping to their broken knees as I toss them into the garbage bag. "If that's the worst thing you did in Europe, it can't be too bad."

"No. But I don't miss Europe."

"That's the first time I've heard you laugh all year, Stacy," Lance comments from the doorway. "Somebody buy this guy a coffee."

"Here, let me help you." Maurice says, grabs the bag of chicken bones and heaves it into the trash. "I can run you home later, no prob. Jared might want another ride in my jalopy before it snows. Separated, eh? A year?"

When I turn my head away, my eyes are swimming. He leans forward, pats my shoulder.

Maurice adopts the habit of driving me home each afternoon before doubling back to Philip's apartment in Hillhurst. I'm glad of the company. Relieved too, that he doesn't hit on me. Friendship, I can bear. He cracks bad jokes and talks non-stop, tells off-colour stories about his cruise ship adventures and European nightclubs. Some days, Jared's bus arrives in front of the apartment just as we pull up, and Jared leaps into the Corvette and insists we go around the block, black gravel spitting like curses behind the car's rear tires. Even though it's months until spring, he's begging for ice cream. I sigh and shrug. Maurice spins us around the corner and insists on buying. Eating ice cream is an act of hope. Maybe this time it will taste like caramel on coffee. But no. My espresso ripple is dull, flat black. Bitter-sweet grape-fruit sorbet for Maurice. Jared is still caught in his infatuation for blue bubblegum. When we get home, azure is smeared across his cheeks like a badge of honour.

Winter arrives. Snow heralds the cold, and I braise Indian lamb shanks and Moroccan goat, simmer chickpea and lentil stews loaded with roasted garlic and leeks, get home from work in the dark, my skin stained orange from turmeric, my mouth still tasting only bitterness, most days arriving to find Jared home ahead of me. He has his own key, my latchkey lad, locks the door right behind himself. I have taken to cooking from books, following instructions to the letter, no longer adventuring, trust gone. Lance says nothing, just raises his eyebrows as he dips his tasting spoons into my pans. But one day I overhear Philip above the hiss of steam from the cappuccino machine.

" . . . used to make the most amazing soup of feta and cinnamon and eggplant, but she stopped. Nothing she makes is as good as it was. I feel sorry for her. And that pinched-off kid of hers — " Maurice says something I can't make out, a low-pitched interruption. "No, she never mentions him. He never comes around."

I drop my sauté pan on the countertop with a clatter. Philip's voice abruptly halts. I poke my head around the end of the cappo machine. "For Chrissake," I mutter.

"What? I was just raving about your cooking, you poor doll. And telling Maurice how that cad hubby of yours just up and left you both high and dry."

Maurice interjects. "Never mind, sweetie. I'll take your kid for ice cream. That'll cheer you both up. And maybe a whisky float for me, I could use a little coddling."

"It's too cold for ice cream, you idiot." But I am laughing, and Maurice is as good as his word.

After school, Jared clamours for ice cream when I mention Maurice. I demur and stay home, drinking herb tea, and shake my head as they enter the apartment, Jared stumbling over the doormat like a clumsy colt, Maurice neat-footed and efficient, cones clenched in their hands.

"We brought you a tub of coconut, Mom, look, it's pee-yellow," Jared giggles.

"Put it in the freezer, you goof. I'll have some after supper."

Another Sunday. My day off. Maurice shows up, raises his thin eyebrows and Jared's jacket is on before they are out the door. I barely look up from my book. I'm reading food science, tomes by Harold McGee and Diane Ackerman, hunting clues on scent and taste.

Half an hour passes before Jared comes back in alone and goes straight to his room.

"Hey, kiddo. Where's my ice cream?" No answer from down the hall. Oh well. There's still sorbet in the freezer. I turn back to the pages of the science book.

Jared's in a funk by supper. I coax and crack bad jokes, but he's morose, insists his dad is sure to drop by, complains about my lentil soup — why don't I ever make dishes that his dad likes?

"What's wrong, sweetie?" I ask, but he kicks the table-leg, fidgets, pulls away from hugs and slices of chocolate tart.

I finally snap at him when he sulks for the fifth morning in a row. He's still sullen when I arrive home in Maurice's Corvette, and it takes effort to convince him say bye when Maurice leaves.

A week later, Maurice blows off his lunch shift. Just before service starts, Philip walks into Lance's office, white and shaking, and emerges a few minutes later with Lance's hand on his shoulder. Philip looks directly at me. "Stacy — " His eyes slide away.

"Not now, Philip." Lance's voice is curt. "Get on the phone, will you, and see if Ian has classes today. Maybe he can work a shift."

I try to catch Philip's eye, but he ducks out to the dining room, then leaves in a flurry of gloves and scarf when lunch is done, so I drag a sack of onions across the tile floor to the counter and start slicing. The rhythm of my knife biting through each orb sends me into a trance that is undisturbed until Lance scrapes his chair across the floor to sit beside my workspace.

My mouth is thick. Finally. This must be it. My cooking has not improved. My mouth still cannot distinguish between spices and sensations, bitterness trumping, but this feeling of fear, this is unmistakable. He is going to fire me.

"Stacy." I ignore him, walk to the back door and pull on my jacket. "Wait! Stacy, what are you doing?"

"Sorry, Lance. I've done my best." My voice is flat.

"Stacy! This is not about you. Well, not directly. It's about Maurice. Sit down."

"Maurice? He didn't come to work. So?"

"Philip says he's been arrested."

"Why? What's wrong? What's he done?"

"The Irish police are starting extradition proceedings. He's been charged with sexual assault." Lance raises his head, looks me straight in the face. "Well, child molestation, actually. A boy. About your Jared's age."

Lance is still speaking but I don't register the words as I fly out the door, cell phone in hand.

Ordinary people look ordinary. So do the less ordinary, with their unusual, un-ordinary hungers. I was naïve, maybe arrogant, but I always assumed that I would be able to identify cruelty. Just by looking. But that sense failed me, too. What did happen is a mother's nightmare, that my blithe unseeing faith in my own radar put my son at risk.

Jared insists that nothing unusual happened between him and Maurice. "Ice cream," he says when the cops ask straight out, repeating it when I ask more hesitantly. "We ate ice cream. That was all." But I watch closely and see how my son holds himself within his body differently, tentatively, as if he is collecting and controlling his memories. Or his hurt. I can't tell which. My prodding and prying might do more harm than good. How can I ever know how much salt to add, when enough is enough?

The blue jay is haunting the feeder as usual this morning. Jared is asleep. He's sleeping later, since Maurice.

When I went back to work after the cops were done talking with my kid, Lance asked me what else was going on. "With your cooking, I mean," he added. He was trying to be gentle, but under my whites my back started to sweat. So I told him. Simple as that. Now Lance is reading his own copies of McGee and Ackerman, and he stands behind me, tasting spoons ready. No recriminations. I wonder if the result would have been the same if it weren't for Maurice. I'd hate to feel anything like gratitude for that man.

The espresso pot's on the stove. Maybe this time my coffee will taste black as night, sweet as sin, bitter as love.

The Pickup Man

TODAY WE'RE GOING TO SEE THE chucks in the desert near Drumheller, at the best small-town rodeo in Alberta. To celebrate, Clarisse is wearing a pink straw cowboy hat, clutching its satin cord around her neck as she spits cherry pits out the open window. I've been teasing her about that hat ever since we rolled outta Calgary, working hard to get a smile out of her, trying to keep her from fretting on our destination. "Lookin' for a cowboy, Clarisse?" I say now. "You, a buckle bunny?"

Before we left Calgary, I promised her that we'd bypass downtown Drumheller. She don't ever want to drive down Main Street. Their house has too much of her blood in the floorboards for her to ever want to see it again. Just before the land dips down into the coulee and we turn east at the water tower above the prison, I see her shiver. I dunno if it's concern for Aidan, facing the dangerous temptations of teen life, or realizing every man locked behind those bars has a wife or mother who's watched his fall. Or knowing Gavin's there in the slammer for a good long time. Looking at the water tower, I feel a river of regret, missing the Gavin I knew as a kid, the big brother who protected me from Dad's fists. That's not the Gavin Clarisse lived with, and she ain't likely to believe me if I describe him to her.

We're quiet until we pull into the parking lot at the rodeo grounds. Aidan gets out of the back seat slowly. I've noticed that, he don't run into things. He holds back and assesses the lay of the land. That sure ain't what I see in most of the teenagers who hang out near the drop-in centre where I work security. Some of them run toward trouble with both arms open.

The parking lot at the top of the coulee has a rail fence and closely cropped grass underfoot. Next to it, a big marquee tent for supper and dancing. The track is on the flatland at the bottom of the hill. It's an open-air place, a natural theatre, wooden benches set into the hillside in a half-moon above the track. When the horses get going, the sound of their hooves will echo from the far wall of the coulee. You can go right down to the rail and hang over, your nose inches from the rigs. Drumheller is the stripped-down version of the Calgary Stampede — if you can cowboy here, you can cowboy anywhere.

I grab a quick look at my watch, then point down the hill to the benches.

"Down there, Aidan. Things don't start 'til four, we've got half an hour yet, but I want you and your mom to meet my boss Linda. I ain't seen as much of you two as I'd like since the move, and workin' for Linda is most of the reason why." I hope I don't sound apologetic even though I mean the words as one, an explanation wrapped in a sunny day spent together. There haven't been enough of 'em for my nephew and me.

He lags behind as I lead Clarisse down the hillside. Her flimsy sandals slip on the grass and I want to scoop her up and carry her. Instead, I grab her right elbow, gentle as I can.

"Thanks, Troy." She don't flinch, just pats my hand, then pulls her arm free.

"Linda, here's my sister-in-law Clarisse and her kid I told you about."

Linda's sharp eyes squint a bit as she gives Aidan, then Clarisse, the one-up-and-down. My boss is surrounded by a gaggle of older gals all dolled up in exactly the same outfit Linda's in. Tooled black leather cowboy boots and bare legs. Denim skirts. Denim jackets, each with orange blossoms stitched on the front, 'Wild Lilies' on the back in swanky red lettering. I watch Clarisse turn that thin neck of hers and study the women sitting in rows, their cushion-softened benches protecting their asses from the desert, and I wonder if those ladies seem like calm laying hens on soft fat roosts to my worn-thin sister-in-law.

"You've never been to the chucks, Clarisse?" Linda asks.

Clarisse turns back to Linda and shakes her head, a narrow movement that flicks her brown hair across her throat. She's finally grown her hair again, the first time in years it's hung past her ears. When Gavin and I met her sixteen years ago, she was a pretty thing, dancing up a storm at the St. Louis bar on the east side of Calgary, her hair in a long braid that swung over her shoulder. She cut it short right after Gavin grabbed her by the braid when she was pregnant with the kid. She never did explain why she chose Gavin over me. Maybe it was my cowboying. Or the booze. But after she cut her hair and I didn't call Gavin on it, I felt I lost the right to even ask.

Linda smiles. "Well, allow me to enlighten you." She hands Clarisse a beer, then lobs ginger ales from a cooler to Aidan and me, the tins beaded with cold. She waves at the women sitting close by. "We're old hands, aren't we, girls? We just love cowboys." Without cuing, a well-padded blonde stands up, turns a Rockettes-type of spin to model her outfit, the other women hooting and hollering. Her skirt rides halfway up her brown thighs. Beside me, I can feel Aidan heat up, eyeing her skirt and fancy boots while Linda snorts, a little like a horse herself. "Chuck wagon drivers are auctioned off each spring," she explains. "We girls, we're all lawyers in Calgary. We all like the Stampede, so five years ago we put together this consortium, we do it every year for the chuckwagon auction. The lucky driver's rig wears our tarp for the length of the circuit. We get the cowboy, he gets us. We'll have worn him out by then, right, girls?"

Clarisse, her hatband stained dark with sweat, perches next to one of the women, who smiles at her and starts telling a story about last year's cowboy, a guy I know from Indian Head, tall dude, the biceps of a farrier. I half-expect Clarisse to make a sideways face at the skanky descriptions of body parts, but she simply laughs, her back slouching into a relaxed curve. I nudge Aidan, slumped between us, his gaze drawn back to the Lilies. "Look, another dumb-ass t-shirt. 'Save fuel. Ride a cowboy.' Ha." He shrugs, but his cheeks are red as he stares at the women.

Linda's a shark, needs to be as the director of the drop-in centre. She and Clarisse are chalk and cheese, but they have the same inner toughness. I've seen Linda roaring like a bear mother, standing up for her cubs. The fact that her cubs are the city's worst-off citizens don't matter none. Linda's stood down nervous cops and stoned-out teenagers twice her size. Just last week, with folks crowding the streets for the Stampede, she walked out in the half-dark of late evening to the benches along the river, and with me at her back, calm as a cuke she talked some guy on crack into letting go of the little girl he'd grabbed. Today she's all slicked up, and even with all the lines on her face, she looks like she was born the same year as Clarisse. I know that ain't so.

Clarisse is at least fifteen years younger — her teeth are knocked crooked from Gavin's beatings, her skin's gone pale with staying indoors, but she's out here, sitting in the sunlight. Laughing.

While we wait for the chucks to get ready, we watch the bull riding. When two men on Quarter horses lope into the ring seconds before a bull erupts from the chutes, Aidan is derisive.

"Two guys riding in circles? For real? It's a joke, right?"

It's the first time the kid's opened his mouth all day. First time I've heard that jeering teenage attitude from him, too. "Don't be a fool," I say. My tone is sharper than I mean. "Those pickup riders saved my life more'n once."

Beside me, Aidan pulls away. Damnation. Didn't mean to scare the kid. Eight seconds later, the horses lope up either side of the plunging bull. One man gets an arm around the bull rider, who swings onto the horse and then to the ground, jumping from a moving rump. The second rider moves his horse close to the wild-eyed bull, reaches down and releases the cinch around its belly with a backhanded flip. Clarisse half-covers her eyes and gasps. She's right. It's scary, but it's poetry.

"All these years," I say to her. "All these years, and I bet this is the first time you actually come to a rodeo."

"Gavin wouldn't let me." Ah. Yeah, Gavin was always jealous. The bugger never bothered getting good at anything, hated to see it in others. Even his own brother. "And now with him gone up, I wanted to see what it is you've been telling me about. All these years," she says, leaving me flat-footed with wonder. Ah, women.

"Every one of those guys has a limp," Aidan observes, oblivious of his mother.

"Yep. Even the rookies walk as if they ache." I clasp my belt buckle. "Bull riders have real jelly bellies, intestinal problems, their guts gone to hell from years of jolts." Aidan examines the ginger ale in my hand, then the bulge where my gut hangs over my leather belt. I nod. "Yep."

"Why'd you quit?"

"Quit what? Drinkin'? Or bulls?"

Aidan shrugs again, his face wooden.

"Ask me straight out if you want a straight answer. To answer — both — it's something about survivin' past thirty." A sideways flicker at Clarisse. She don't notice, she's so caught up in watching the horses in the ring. "At my age, it's better to be the pickup man." Aidan scrunches his nose in confusion. I relent and sigh. "I've told you before, bud. About the bull tried to take my eye out." I lower my voice and lean closer to him so Clarisse can't hear. "Makes a guy think twice. The girls might not think I'm so sexy if I wore an eye patch. Or worse." I hitch at my jeans. His eyes widen. A few minutes later, I catch him looking reflectively at his mother, and I'm guessing he's totting up the black eyes and split lips.

A breeze rolls in, clouds tumbling and roiling as the afternoon slides by.

"Gonna rain," says Aidan, tilting his face skyward.

"Hours yet, honey," Clarisse says. "Put on your ballcap. You'll get burnt." She leans back, puts her feet up on the empty bench in front of her. Aidan drops an arm over her shoulder. She turns to me. "Did I tell you how I got this hat?"

"No. What's so special about it? Other'n bein' a cowboy hat and pink, and makin' you look cute as a button."

"Cut it out, Troy."

"Sorry. Tell the story."

"The week we moved to Calgary, I went downtown to The Bay and I saw it in the window. So I bought it. For myself." She stops and waits.

I have a swift full-colour image in my head of Clarisse in pink satin shirt and jeans, striding into the department store, setting off firecrackers and yodelling while she lassoes a pink straw hat from a mannequin. She might have done it as a teenager.

"I don't get it. What's the big deal about a hat?"

"Gavin always took all my wages, Troy. I had enough for groceries and what Aidan needed. Nothing for me. Not until . . ."

I remember that she'd wore the same faded blouses for years. Remember too that Lora's offers of castoff dresses never got took up.

"Honey, the hat's just great. I know you ain't a buckle bunny."

She looks at me, perplexed for half a heartbeat, then she laughs, head back, crooked teeth shining in her wide mouth.

An hour later, the calves and ropers are rounded up and gone, and the clouds are rolling in. The first four chuckwagons line up on the track. The Wild Lilies surge to their feet. I follow them as they rush down to the rail and hang over its edge. They whoop and holler some more, cheering their driver and his four-horse hitch, three tons of horseflesh, sixteen hooves, all controlled with leather reins thinner'n my pinky. On the track, one outrider holds the lead horses' bridles while the other heaves the camp-stove into the back of the rig. His partner turns loose the lead horses, then they both vault into their own saddles and the rig is in high gallop, carving a figure eight round the barrels, thundering around the track. A half-mile of hell, it's been called, a dozen guys, on rigs and in the saddle. Takes a certain kinda crazy that reminds me of my days on the bulls.

The horses' nostrils up close are red and wide, the track churned into chaos under their tearing hooves. They sound like the trains we used to hear from our house in Drumheller. They sound like fists on flesh. I look around, my mouth dry, looking for Clarisse, and recall arriving in the yard of Gavin and Clarisse's house two years ago as a train rumbled up the track. My brother strolled past me and out the gate, threading his belt into the loops on his jeans. I got inside in double time and found her on the kitchen floor. When she saw me, she pulled herself into a sitting position, her hand clutching her nose, blood seeping between her fingers. "I hate the sound of those trains," she said, her voice muffled. "Don't, Troy. I can do it." She stood up, shook off my help, her back straight as she walked to the bathroom.

"Clarisse," I say, hardly aware I've climbed the hill to stand in front of her where she sits alone. "Are you all right? I hate to see — "

She smiles at me, her face in bloom. "Of course I'm all right. Still looking out for me after all these years!"

That resets my stopwatch. I turn away and take my seat without saying nothing else. Looking out for her. Hell, even the flirting's become so second nature that I guess I'd expected a little sugar.

Aidan noiselessly slides past me onto the bench beside her, slips his hand in hers as if he was a kid again, his eyes flicking from his mother to me and back to her. Minutes crawl by without anyone saying a word. I'm relieved when the heat's times are announced and the Wild Lilies down at the rail erupt, jangling their bracelets and yowling like cats in heat. Linda prances up to us and plants a kiss on Aidan's cheek. Even his ears turn bright red.

"Did you win?" Clarisse asks, on her feet and clapping.

"We had the fastest time in our heat. The rest of the heats have yet to run, but points accumulate all season." Linda plunks herself down and pats the bench beside Clarisse. "It'll be awhile before supper. So tell me all about what you're doing with yourself."

Their voices are drowned out as more horses thunder around the track. The Lilies stay put, their horses done for the day. Another hour passes. I watch the beer cooler empty. I'm still thinking on Clarisse's words when she tugs at my shirtsleeve.

"Linda knows a good dentist," she half-shouts, raising her voice over the high-pitched laughter of the Lilies. "He's done stuff for some of her people, takes payment over time, she says. Good rates."

"Yeah?" I almost yell in her ear. "That's really great, Clarisse." It'll be another step toward repairing the marks of Gavin's temper. More proof she don't need my arm to catch her. I know I should be glad, but somehow I'm not.

The noise level climbs. By nine, as the final heat concludes, the clouds let loose.

"Ladies! Let's beat the rain *and* the supper crowds!" Linda abandons her beer on the bench and hustles her girls up the hill. Aidan eyeballs the can and tries to snag it without Clarisse noticing.

"You hungry, Aidan?" I grab his arm, knock the can over and out of reach, tow him up the grassy slope, my other arm around Clarisse to protect her from the rain.

The banners draped on the tent's central peak are whipping as the breeze picks up. A band is tuning onstage under the spotlights, sounding tinny. When the fiddler breaks into the opening bars of "Your Cheatin' Heart," the floor fills. The three of us weave through the swarm of bodies, collect potato salad and smokies on buns, lean against the metal doorjamb to watch. The Lilies are celebrating their rig's first-place standing after the evening's heats, a gaggle clustered across the dance floor. Even from here I can hear 'em cracking blue jokes about their driver.

A grey-haired couple in dancing duds two-steps past, light-footed as ropers in their best boots. She smiles like a girl when her eyes meet mine. Aidan points at a young guy in an old-timey wide-brimmed hat, twirling his date, catching and tossing her like the roping is still going on. "Those old dudes are better than that hotshot," he says.

"They've been dancing together a long time, I bet," I say lightly. As if time solves everything.

Across the marquee, a blonde in boots and a thigh-high skirt breaks free from the Lily patch and spots us. "One of Linda's buckle bunnies," I whisper. Clarisse pokes me in the ribs, her nails sharp. The blonde pushes through the pack until she stands, hands on hips, in front of us, then grabs Aidan by the arm without noticing his flinch.

"Come on, kid. I'll teach you how to two-step." She tugs him onto the crowded floor to the strains of "Someday Soon" just as the suns slides out of the clouds and sets. He stumbles beside her, then in the next step, he gets it, leaning into the rhythm, his arms relaxed. Clarisse, jammed beneath my arm, claps and whistles when Aidan, spinning by, grins at us, a blaze of teeth.

"He's great!" she yells, and gives him a thumbs-up. We watch them turn and dip around the floor until the song ends, when Aidan half-bows to the blonde before he disappears into the crowd.

The band cuts into "Pancho and Lefty," and I'm leaning down, about to ask Clarisse to dance, when a redhead stops beside us, her breath sweet with whisky. Do I know her face? One of Gavin's many cast-offs, maybe. "You seen my daughter? Long hair? About this tall?"

Clarisse shakes her head. I nudge her, my face turned aside. "Where are the outriders? She should look there."

The drunken mother leans in to listen. Her face slackens, then tenses. "She's thirteen!" she hisses.

I get a good look at her. "Rose?" I say, recognizing her too late, from my days as a bouncer at the Drumheller Hotel. "You lookin' for Judith?" Knowing the missing girl, a kid younger than Aidan, I realize what a blockhead I musta sounded. My apology is drowned by the storm's arrival, the tent's canvas walls flapping in the wind. I set Clarisse on a chair, shepherd Rose to the line-up for the ladies' with a promise to find her lost girl, and hustle back help the guys shift tables away from the walls dripping rain. Yellow air, soil on the move, unstoppable and gritty, like Pop's wasted years rolling east, lives blowing away.

The wind quits, the rain stopping as quick as it started. The clouds part to reveal a sickle moon, orange in the cooling air. Down the hillside, on the bleachers, I can see two figures, the small frame of a girl, a blonde braid dangling down her back, leaning against the taller one. Then I recognize the shape of the head next to her as Clarisse moves soundlessly to my side.

"Down there," I say, and point, then kick myself as soon as the words leave my mouth. A boy's first moments with a girl are fragile, best kept private, away from his mother's eyes. Clarisse's skinny hand tenses on my forearm.

I turn to her. "He's a good kid, Clarisse. So's that little girl, I've known her mom for years. Nothing's gonna happen."

"This storm, the noise, it's unnerving. Reminds me of Gavin, and I start worrying that he's somehow rubbed off on Aidan."

"What? Aidan don't have a mean bone. He never has. He's had you all these years. That counts for lots."

"Just check. Please, Troy. I'd go down there myself, but I don't want to embarrass him."

"Okay, okay. I'll tell him it's time to push off." I set off, still nimble despite my limp. The kids don't hear me, are giggling when I reach them. I change my footing, bring my boots down like I mean business. Aidan turns around, pulls away from the girl.

"Uncle Troy!"

"Hey, Aidan."

"Hey. Mom okay?"

"She needs you." I nod to the girl. "You're Judith, right? I know your mom. She's lookin' for ya."

"She's drunk," the girl sneers, twisting her braid between her fingers. "She's always drunk."

"She's sad, girlie. Something happened to break her joy. You gotta remember she loves you."

The girl's face narrows and tightens. "Yeah? And who are you? Who made you the big guardian?"

"I guess I did that myself. Go find your mom, honey. It's almost ten o'clock and I need to talk to Aidan here."

She makes an ugly face at me, and kicks at the wet grass. "What if Aidan doesn't want me to go?"

"I think Aidan might call you next week. Right, Aidan?" His puzzled look, then his nod and wide-ass grin a couple seconds later. "I know your mom," I remind her, "I'll see he gets your number."

She trails slowly up the hill. "Oh, all right. Bye, Aidan."

"Bye."

"Don't forget," she says over her shoulder, directed at both of us.

I wait until Aidan turns to face me. "Your mom's joy is busted too, Aidan. She needs your help to put things back together." I watch, worrying. Wondering if he'll ape the girl he just met, and diss his mother. I can see the thought flicker in his eyes.

He angles away, faces up the slope. "You're not my dad."

"No, I'm not." I'm sorry Aidan has mentioned Gavin. What can I say that Aidan hasn't already learned the hard way? I know if I have to, I'll play my brother, the soiled and sticky trump card in my tattered deck of tricks. Somehow this small moment beneath the orange moon has become something larger, and I wonder if Aidan understands what's going down. He stares pokerfaced at me, his father's face ghosting over his features, and I see exactly how my nephew will look as a man.

"So you can't tell me what to do."

I give him a little room, follow when he heads up the hill, my boot heels muffled on the wet grass.

"You like my mom," he mutters. I can barely hear him.

"Yep. I do."

"I mean, you *like* her."

For the second time this evening, I'm pole-axed. I've put my feeling for Clarisse behind me. What did Aidan see, if I put it behind me?

"You're wrong, Uncle Troy. Mom's not broken." His voice is sharp. "She doesn't need you. She needs me."

My boots slip on the grass. Beneath my belt, my rebellious guts seethe.

"What do you do for fun now?" Aidan asks. "Do you miss the bulls? Riding them, I mean?" He sounds like a guitar string about to break.

I stop on the hillside. Recall Linda, standing down the doper on the riverbank. Clarisse, buying a pink cowboy hat and finding a new home. And now Aidan, two-stepping like a man. "Nah. Not anymore," I finally say. "There's lots of thrills, most of 'em way safer now that I'm an old dude. Compared to you young bucks, I mean. We'll talk about it more, yeah? I'll come get you from school after work next week, take you out for coffee. Just you and me, eh? We've got lots to talk about." In my head, I see Gavin, stepping into the hall, leaving me safe in the closet. Aidan should know that side of his dad too.

"Yeah," he says, his voice shaky.

By the time Aidan and I reach the truck, we're both calm, and Clarisse has the AC and "High Lonesome Sound" cranked up for the drive home in the darkness.

Other Mothers' Sons

THE BOY WAS SITTING AT THE lip of the TransCanada Highway, thumb out, the elephant-hide hills east of Kamloops behind him. He held a hand-lettered sign. *Please.* The tarmac wavered in the heat. Joanna started to brake as she read the single word, then searched for a turnaround point, but backtracking on the highway is never simple. By the time she'd found a safe place to carve her first U-turn, then another a good five miles back the way she'd come, ten minutes had elapsed before she pulled her car to a stop in the shale at the young man's feet.

She lowered the passenger window, doors still locked, and took a careful look. The kid's backpack was Army surplus, his work boots and khaki shorts coated with dust and smudged with grit. His face was clean. "Hop in," she said, and hit the unlock button. He nodded at her, his hands busy with door handle and seat belt clasp, but his eyes said thanks from beneath the bandana wrapped around his forehead, biker style. A few miles later, she heard him sigh and sensed his body relaxing into the seat.

There was no need to ask where he was headed. East. No other roads. No other direction. No map needed. She was grateful to not think, not feel, to simply react to the needs of the highway, her own body slackening in response to the regular breathing next to her. That was familiar too, and she trusted her reaction. She slid "Motherland" into the slot, turned it down low and let the road unwind, the gypsy-like violins and mandolin a counterpoint to the steep terrain.

The engine's gears revved as she shifted on the winding road along Shuswap Lake. Cornering, lake visible beyond, she glanced at him. He was no more than sixteen. Stocky. Tanned. A thick fringe of bleached blond hair hung over his eyes, the rest buried beneath the bandana. The white wires of an iPod dangled from his hoodie's neckline, and a well-creased topographical map, its black lines concentric s- and omega-curves, protruded from the hoodie's kangaroo pocket at the wire's end. For as long as it took her eyes to flicker from the road to his face and back to the road, she imagined Ryan lounging in the seat, his favourite position on their trips for summer fruit, sandaled feet up on the transom, long brown hair tossing as he turned his head to study the landscape. Joanna blinked the image away.

The boy slept while she gassed up in Three Valley Gap, slept during the long climb into Revelstoke, woke as she approached the high curved bridge above the gorge outside of Golden. Joanna heard him shifting on the seat beside her, but the overpass held her gaze. A lot of her inner attention had been focused on death the past few years, but not hers, and not here. Confronting the possibilities, of gaping space beyond the tiny and totally insufficient safety rail, of riding a diving, twisting wreck from such a height, was graphic enough, doubly so now that she had some other mother's son in the car.

"Where are we?" He sounded as rusty as she was at talking to teenagers.

"Golden. Near the border. A map's in the glovebox." He didn't bother looking, just stretched, the slight pop and crack of his vertebrae drowned out by the growling of his stomach. "You hungry?" He nodded. "There's a case of peaches and a cooler behind you. Can you reach either? Help yourself."

He swivelled within the embrace of the seatbelt. His groping fingers emerged from the cooler's depths clutching a tub. "What's this stuff?" Joanna, risking another glance, saw forearms, tanned, muscular, blue corded veins tensing in the backs of his hands. For half a heartbeat, she wondered if she had made a mistake in breaking her own cardinal rule of travelling alone — no hitchhikers, ever — but the look of gratitude as he straightened in the seat reassured her. This was a kid who needed feeding, no rapist, no threat at all. And hadn't she been pushing weights and taking fitness classes all her life? Surely if anything happened, she could defend herself against a hungry kid. She shook her head in amazement. How'd she get there so quickly? From pity to self-preservation in half a blink. Whoa, Jo.

"Curried chicken. Try it. What's your name?"

"Bobbie. Bob."

"I'm Joanna. Where's home?"

"Lethbridge. Going back to my Granny. Been gone all summer."

"Doing what?" Granny. Not Mom. Or dad, either. Joanna felt like a dentist, extracting chips of old molar and prodding at invisible cavities. Having this lad in her car tipped her straight back into parent mode.

"Tree-planting." Half a pause as he tipped his head north. "I look older than I am." He sounded defensive.

"I'm going as far as Calgary," she said, then directed him to a plastic plate, fork and napkin in the cooler's saddlebag. The muffled sound of eating. Maybe days since he'd eaten last. Joanna remembered Ryan's prodigious appetite before his illness, the plateloads of pasta at supper, how his upper body would disappear into the fridge two hours later, then emerge and straighten, smiling, hands full. She'd shopped for apples by the case, cheese by the wheel. Then nearly overnight, nothing she'd cooked interested him, his body fading, skin paling, then headaches that he'd said were cracking his skull from the inside. Thinking back, she recalled her own youthful hitchhiking expeditions, filled with hunger and heat, the long hot wait in dust for the hiss of airbrakes and a ride home. It had felt like a safer world then. Or she'd been lucky.

She gestured at the water bottle by the boy's knee. He nodded, swigged, offered it to her.

"Calgary," she said, renewing the conversation. "I can drop you at the bus depot."

His face coloured. "I'll just hitch," he said. "Cheaper." He was asleep again within ten minutes, the bottle rattling in the footwell by his knee.

Joanna drove through the evening, her window cracked partly open. She leaned her head on the glass and counted the tunnels as they unzipped around the car, gorges falling away to the valley far below. No matter how many times she drove this road, it still caught her breath. Something about the explorers. David Thompson. Simon Fraser. How had they found their way through this narrow high pass? Just dumb luck? Following rivers or native guides? Or did they imagine the maps before they drew them, the valleys opening into the unfamiliar? That was difficult to conceive; she could never see what was coming, hadn't suspected the worst until she walked cold and unsuspecting into her son's hospital room to hear his doctor's verdict. A fever, she'd thought, the flu. How quickly his body had shut down. Weeks. Invaded by the unknown.

Twilight faded into blackness. At the Continental Divide, she cranked open the sunroof. Above her head, stars twinkled like handfuls of gemstones. A few miles later, a glimpse of the eerie dancing of the northern lights. Beside her, the kid slept, his left arm twitching in a dreamer's trance, his head tipped back against the headrest.

No other cars were on the road. She pulled over and stopped, reached for a peach from the full case on the back seat. She glanced at the boy, wondering if he looked like his mother. If she missed him. Surely. The borealis leaped from sky to windshield, the sky baroque and wild and beautiful. The boy slept on, his head rolling, unaware of Joanna beside him, her head thrown back, looking and weeping for what she could never hold again. When her eyes dried, she tossed the peach pit, released the brake, let out the clutch, eased back onto the road. For the first time in nearly two years, she wondered where Stuart was. The divide between them had unobtrusively widened, and when her husband packed his bags and moved into an apartment Joanna had barely noticed.

It was three AM when they crossed Calgary's city limits. Joanna thought again about the bus depot. It would be bright, glaring with fluorescent lights and the dark smell of lateness and hard travel. Strangers would be milling at the doors, smoking, hanging out, suspicious. And here she sat, worrying about this unfamiliar child, someone else's child. Not her dead son.

The kid stirred. Joanna saw tree saplings in the curve of his cheek and new leaves in the flutter of his eyelashes, and wheeled her car through the sleeping city to her front yard.

She reached out, hesitant again, then tapped his shoulder. "We're home."

He fumbled with the car door and his pack while Joanna quickly moved past him and unlocked the bungalow. In the hall, she opened a door. "You can sleep in here."

Ryan's room was as he had left it when he took that final trip to the hospital, robin-blue paint chipping beneath the corners of his Davie Bowie posters. Just seeing the chips brought back the ache. Not tonight. No unpacking those memories. How many things did she avoid thinking and feeling this way? She never did unpack them. It felt safer to keep the trunk locked, the key safely out of sight, and when tomorrow arrived, she invariably tucked the memories behind the day's doings. Keeping busy filled days she didn't want to count. Eight months after the funeral Stuart had gently suggested another baby, but Joanna had shivered, cried and pushed him away. No one could replace Ryan. She didn't understand how he could carry on as if nothing had been lost. As if the world hadn't fallen off the map, into the realm of the unimaginable.

"The bathroom's down there. There's a spare toothbrush in the drawer." The kid blearily stumbled into the bathroom, the door closing on his small night noises.

Joanna collapsed on her own bed, her body slowly letting go of car springs and the roar of air through car windows. She lay still until she heard the bathroom door squeak, then decided against flossing and fell into dreamless sleep.

Joanna woke early. The boy's face appeared through the kitchen door as she drank her first coffee.

"Your son. He been gone long?"

"Almost three years. He was about your age. Leukemia."

"Sorry."

"Yeah. I still wake up thinking he'll be at the breakfast table."

The boy ducked his head. She set out cereal, sliced peaches, bowl and spoon, milk. He ate without another word. She ate yogurt and peach slices, finished her coffee. Phrases rolled like guttering bowling balls. "Did you finish your algebra? Don't forget your trumpet, band class today. How about we make chicken cacciatore again for supper?"

Joanna flipped on the computer and checked the Greyhound schedule. "If we leave right now, you can just catch the nine-forty. Can you manage?"

His face reddened as he shook his head. "I thought I'd hitch."

"The trip's on me." She angled away slightly as he muttered his thanks. "It's okay. Time to go."

No talking as they got in the car. It was late August, the sun already high in the sky at nine AM. The street under her car's wheels sang, the clear note of summer passing at each corner she crossed, the roads opening into other possibilities, other lives. She could smell the trees through the window, their arms bright and pale green like naiads along the riverbank. The heavy wetness of earth and water, the solid, unwavering line where they met. Here, there. Before, now.

Joanna handed him two peaches when the car stopped rolling in the parking lot. "Take these for the trip." She led the way down the stairs into the bus depot. "One way to Lethbridge. Student, right?" She laid her credit card on the counter and gestured at the boy. He fumbled in his wallet, found his student ID card.

"Listen, thanks, eh." He was standing at the door into the bus barn. She couldn't follow.

She nodded, grabbed his wrist briefly, shouldered away, left him framed by the high light of morning as she headed to the stairs.

On her way out of the parking lot, the car pointed west along the river, she saw the back of a denim jacket and began to brake. As she rolled past, she swivelled her head and stared.

He was standing in the median, a brunet, like Ryan. Long hair tipped in gold, the ends visible under his straw cowboy hat. Red sleeve, the edge of his Smithbilt, stained. And the sign in his hands, half visible past the intercepting light standard. She strained to read the word in the morning light's glare. *Change?*

She gunned the motor and spun gravel as she drove past. Change. It came whether you wanted it or not, often bitter, only occasionally sweet, rarely controllable. A map taking a blind, unexpected turn.

She could smell the perfume of the ripe peaches in the back of the car. Why had she bought an entire case?

When Joanna reached the house, she carried the case of fruit into the kitchen, then slowly walked the hall into Ryan's room, opened the closet, stood staring at the empty boxes stacked on the floor, his clothing undisturbed, shirts hanging, sleeves in straight creased drops from sloping shoulders. Jeans. Hoodies. A photo album in a cardboard banker's box caught her eye, the mattress yielding beneath her as she pulled the book free, pages falling open in her hands. Ryan's face, his long limbs, his gut-busting smile. The strange boy's face reflected in the bus window, safely turned toward home and his Granny. Ryan's face again. She wanted to recall everything about him, then and there, keep it all clear, his lifeline from birth to death.

She set the album on the dresser and picked Ryan's favourite red shirt from a hanger. Folded its arms, slowly, one then the other, across the breast of the faded fabric.

Needful Things

WHEN THE SEWING MACHINE'S NEEDLE BROKE for the third time, Susan dug around in the bulky corduroy with her pliers, grumbling as she searched for the tip. Cutting down the jacket was proving more trouble than it was worth, but the young horse-woman who'd brought it to her had insisted. A gift from her brother, she said. And now Susan was late getting it done.

Each morning, Susan lay in bed and counted the flocked lilies on the wallpaper and considered the temperature of the linoleum. Wondered if she wanted coffee or tea. But she didn't want anything, so each morning she stayed under the duvet. Counting wallpaper flowers. Even her appetite stayed dormant. Eventually, it was her body's discomfort that drove her out of bed, not the urge to step into her day, not the tedious job of re-sizing a jacket.

What was it this jacket reminded her of? Nothing stayed with her for long these days. Not even her garden, where she and Peter had spent their summers. As his health had declined his energy slipped too, but he'd still loved mornings ensconced in a deck chair, watching her dig.

She should finish the damn jacket. If she had to endure one more call from Lauren without new income to report, she might as well stay in bed permanently. Go to sleep for good. Not that she hadn't considered that already. A few extra sleeping pills and some vodka to smooth the way. That she *had* considered, on some lonely Sunday evenings. The daily phone calls didn't help. Prying about money. Her health. Even suggesting Susan see a shrink. "There's no cure for widowhood," she'd told Lauren curtly. "Kindly let me be."

What was the name of that movie? Diane Keaton's vests and neckties. Woody Allen as a morose comedian. Movie nights with Peter on the couch beside her, hogging the popcorn bowl. His absence was an ache that all the daughters in the world couldn't bridge. If she moved to Calgary, she could watch movies with Lauren. She pursed her lips and bent to the sewing machine. Would she take this reliable old Elna Supermatic with her, her last vestige of independence? Even asking the question made her stomach heave. What was left for her here? Her business worn threadbare after ten years of caring for Peter. The neighbours had stopped visiting when she abandoned their weekly coffee klatches. Even Peter's school colleagues had fallen by the wayside.

The doorbell rang just as Susan stabbed the thread through the needle's eye.

"Dammit! Get that, Peter, would you?" Almost said it out loud. She listened for the sound of slippers scuffling down the hall. The house was silent.

She caught herself, cursed, got up to answer the bell. He'd been dead three years.

"Good afternoon. I understand you are a seamstress." A voice flowed from the porch, from a shivering woman clutching a tote bag. Beyond her, the delphiniums craned downward; beyond them, the dishevelment of the last poppies and bachelor buttons.

"Yes, yes, I'm a seamstress," Susan said, pointed at the framed fabric sign Lauren had made. A fanciful thing, hand-quilted treadle with embroidered needles as vertical bars in each letter. The woman hesitated. "Come in then." Susan ushered her in, then stepped back for a quick appraisal. She was shorter than Susan, elliptical, brown-skinned, a thick black braid, a trench coat snugged high, a pink and orange silk scarf peeking from the neckline. "Take your coat?"

"No, thank you." The woman clutched it. "I don't think I will ever get used to how very cold it is here." She placed her palms together. Bowed. "It is good of you to see me without an appointment. I am Yasmina Singh."

"Susan Luckett." Susan snatched her hand back from open air, rubbing her palms. "Yasmina. Pretty name. Sounds like jasmine."

"Exactly that, yes."

"Right. What can I do for you, Jasmine? Here, sit down." She grabbed several blouses and a sweater from the couch. Yasmina unbuttoned her coat, perched on the edge and surveyed the room. The scent of roses drifted from her body. Susan winced as the woman's face registered heaps of DVDs, a clutter of used mugs on the coffee table, and beyond the hallway door, dishes overflowing the kitchen sink. She'd gotten used to eating in front of the television since — since when? Since Lauren grew up and left home? Since Peter's death? Since doing dishes no longer seemed important. The room felt empty, echoing.

"I need a new suit. May I show you?" At Susan's nod, Yasmina opened her purse and pulled out a folded paper, gold and red jewelled bangles tinkling at her wrist. "Here is a photograph."

Susan unfolded the paper and studied the picture. "I don't know any of this." She looked at the clothing visible through Yasmina's gaping coat. "But you're wearing western clothes. This is special?"

Yasmina smiled. "Yes. I've been in Canada for over twenty years. But these clothes — *salwar, kameez,* and a *dupatta,* the scarf — this is traditional Indian clothing. I will wear them in the Gurdwara."

"What's that, the Gurdwara?"

"The temple."

"Hmm. Those clothes look comfortable. Pretty, too. Hmmm. Maybe you can find someone else. Alterations, now, or a hemming job, I could help you with."

"I am remarrying."

Susan flinched and handed back the photograph. "I wouldn't know where to start. And I'd not want to let you down for such an important day, Jasmine. Sorry."

"But my cousin insists that you are very good. The best seamstress in town, she said. The best with silks. Of course it is unlikely you would remember her, she hired you some years ago."

Susan shook her head, halfway to opening the door when a flood of fabric tumbled through Yasmina's hands. Green. Utter green, forest, then jade. Gold threads caught and glittered as the light shifted. Purple glowed along the weft, a hint of rust hiding in its depths.

"Oh my," Susan breathed. "May I?" She gestured toward the fabric.

"Yes, please."

Susan plunged her hands into the run of colours and sighed. When she looked up, Yasmina was watching her, amusement crinkling the faint lines beside her eyes. Brown, shot with amber and gold. Unusual eyes. "What exactly do you need?"

"A suit, as I said. Two pieces. And a long scarf to cover my head." Yasmina held out the photo again. "In joyous colours, as you see. Remarrying is sacred, but meant to be a celebration." She watched closely as Susan studied the garb in the picture.

"Those bottoms are like pajamas, aren't they? And that blouse, a tunic, really. Such sleeves! They're like bells! Did you bring a pattern?"

"I thought you would know."

"I'd have to draft something. It's been a long time." Susan hesitated. "This is all so strange to me. Maybe we should just forget about it." She thrust the fabric at Yasmina. "No. I don't think so."

The woman's face folded in. "I understand. You do not like to make foreign clothes. My cousin said — "

"No, that's not it at all! I just — " Susan waved her hands at her house. "It's too much just now."

"I see." Yasmina tucked the cloth into her tote, held out a card. "Here is my number. Please call if you change your mind."

The scent of roses had faded when the phone bleated.

"Lauren?"

"Mom, I've been looking at condos. Want to fly out this weekend?"

"I don't know. Maybe."

"What's keeping you in Saskatoon? I can't keep worrying like this. Half the time you don't even answer when I phone!"

"It's just too much effort some days."

"Exactly. I hate to think of you lying there on the couch, forgetting to eat. It's a good time to sell, and there are some cute condos on the market in Calgary. If you move here, we could go shopping, and you could have Sunday dinner with Merrill and me."

"Merrill might get sick of seeing his mother-in-law. This place has been home for so long. And there's the garden."

"You need company."

"I'll think about it, okay?"

Lauren sighed. "I'll call you later."

After hanging up, Susan stretched out on the couch, shoving at the tangle of clothing with her feet. She gazed at the fading flowers on the other side of the window and went to sleep.

The phone woke her. "Mom?"

"What?"

"Make some supper."

Susan dropped the phone on the couch, sat up and examined the jacket where she had left it. She squinted at the new seams, then the fabric dissolved into the rippling silk of that afternoon. What beauty could you make with such stuff? She went to her bookshelf, pulled out a well-thumbed book and flipped to the index, muttering under her breath. "Silk, Indian . . . " She curled up on the couch and started to read. Three pages later, she picked up her phone and dialled.

The voice on the other end sounded like bells chiming. "This is Yasmina Singh."

Yasmina's body proportions were challenging. Susan walked around her new client appraisingly, studying her contours, like a soft hillside, hips and waist and breasts all the same dimensions. The tailor's task of measurement felt like an intrusion into a foreign landscape.

After she'd called Yasmina, Susan had washed dishes, sorted laundry, shelved books, re-stacked DVD cases. She had ratcheted a broom from the jumbled closet, and the floor reappeared. It had been after midnight when she'd finally gone to bed.

"Why did you change your mind, Susan?" Yasmina asked.

Susan stopped, the measuring tape loose in one hand. "That fabric, so startlingly lovely. The idea of drafting a pattern again." She fitted her tape along Yasmina's arm, considering. "Making something new." It helped, she'd learned, to keep the client talking. Chitchat for relaxation. "Are you a film buff?"

"What do you mean?"

"A movie fan." Susan nodded towards the DVDs. "Films. *Doctor Zhivago? Lawrence of Arabia?*"

"Oh, movies! Yes. Bollywood is famous for singing and dancing." She chuckled. "I have to admit I prefer English movies. Period pieces. I love *Sense and Sensibility*, with Emma Thompson. My daughter calls them historical soap operas. But she likes documentaries."

As she dropped to her knees to position the tape at Yasmina's ankle, Susan recalled measuring Peter for his fiftieth birthday present. A velvet and satin smoking jacket, blue and purple. He had loved to slide into it each evening, then perch at the kitchen counter, slowly bending into his book. The last piece she'd made. She'd brought the jacket home and hung it in the closet after the funeral, and after that, accepted only alterations and mending, dull work that dulled her needles.

Yasmina pointed at a photo on the wall, Lauren at ten in a Scheherazade costume. "Is that your daughter?"

"Yes. Lauren as a little girl."

"She looks like you."

Susan rolled up the tape measure. "Tales of the Arabian Nights," she said. "Is that where you're from, Jas — so sorry — Yasmina?"

A small snuffle that sounded like relief. Then that musical voice. "No. That is Baghdad. Iraq. We are from Punjab. The city of Ludhiana, in northwest India. But there is very fine silk in Iraq." Another snuffle. "Your daughter is lovely."

"I hardly ever see her. She sells houses in Calgary. Once while I was visiting her, she took me to a fabric store in the northeast. When we finished shopping, we went to an Indian sweet shop. I had my first chai."

"Chai?"

"Would you like some tea? I'll put the kettle on."

"Oh no! That is too much bother. Do not, just for me."

"No trouble."

"I am a customer, I do not expect chai while we discuss business."

"All right. Suit yourself." Susan thought she saw disappointment in Yasmina's eyes, just a flicker of light across the irises. "You want the same neckline as the top you showed me?"

Yasmina's nails gleamed on the fine weave of the sweater at her throat. "Modest, please. One must be decorous in the Gurdwara, where the wedding ceremony will be."

She still looked disappointed, Susan decided. "Wait here." She got up from the couch and went into the kitchen. When she returned, she bore a small plate heaped with gingersnaps. "You must eat something." A half-smile and half-bow as Yasmina nibbled. Reassured, Susan wrote up the measurements beside her sketches and handed Yasmina the sheet to inspect. "Did I get everything?"

She scrutinized the paper, then Susan's hand. "You are married?"

"He's. Gone."

"Widowed?"

Susan's pencil snapped between her fingers. Yasmina's voice quickened. "Oh, my apologies for intruding. My sympathies." Susan shook her head, scrambled for the pencil shards. "My husband was an engineer," Yasmina said. "He has been gone many years." She paused. "Forgive my intruding. It will ease. Eventually." Susan stuffed the bits of pencil into her pocket. Couldn't look up. Was relieved to hear Yasmina's melodic voice resume. "Our daughter, too, will be an engineer. She is studying here, in her third year of university."

"And your fiancé?"

"Like me. A biologist. I study water. We are both professors." She laughed. "Although here where winter lasts so long, it seems I spend more time studying ice than water!"

"Water? You mean water pollution?"

"No. Where water comes from, how long it resides in a watershed system, and the kind of water plants use. Water that ends up in streams is different from water used by plants, most likely as a result of plant-based transpiration and photosynthesis." She caught herself, chuckled. "My undergrad opening lecture. My apologies. Useful things to know. We're like water. Changed by living in the world." A shrug. "My daughter likes water, too. She wants to build bridges."

Susan glanced out the window to the yard, where the saskatoons and mountain ashes were scattering crimson leaves and berries. "Lauren keeps telling me that Calgary is just an hour away. But she never comes. And now she's after me to move there. I think I'm going to have to."

"Why?"

Susan stared speechlessly at her, her mind blank.

Susan spent two days bent over her layout table, painstakingly drafting patterns. Her first attempts struck her as clumsy novice's work, but she finally laid the paper cut-outs on top of the filmy material for the tunic, hesitated, then lay down her pincushion and re-measured each dimension. She paused again, scissors in hand, once every pin was in place. Extra fabric tumbled from table to floor, a waterfall of shifting light. What would it feel like to wear gossamer?

She began to snip. When the phone rang, she let it go unanswered.

After breakfast the next morning, Susan assessed the tea in her cupboard, then she opened the laptop. "All right, mister Google, tell me about chai." A few minutes later, she dropped her glasses in her pocket, pulled on her jacket and strode out of the house.

She had barely returned from the supermarket when the phone buzzed. "Is that you, Lauren?"

"Mom! Where have you been? Are you all right?"

"Of course I'm all right. I went grocery shopping, bought some spices."

"Wow, that's great you're cooking again! You sound so cheerful. But why haven't you called?"

"Work, honey. I'll tell you later."

As Susan hung up, the bedraggled delphiniums caught her eye.

Susan was crouched in the front yard, clipping the deadwood delphinium stalks, when Yasmina strolled up the walk to the porch. The edges of a yellow tunic protruded beneath her quilted vest and jacket, Susan greeted her palms-together bow with a slight inclination of her head.

"This is nice," she said, pulled off her gloves to finger the tunic's hem uninvited. "Good cotton. Maybe some chai before the fitting?" She led the way into the house.

"Chai would be lovely." Yasmina tugged off her jacket and vest, seated herself and glanced around the tidy kitchen.

"Darjeeling. That's Indian, isn't it?" Susan asked, all at once unsure as she plugged in the kettle.

"Most certainly."

"Star anise. Cloves. Nutmeg. Cardamom and cinnamon?" Yasmina nodded as the phone rang. Susan turned her face away. "Lauren? I have a client here."

"I just need a minute. I've booked you a flight." Lauren's voice revved like a racecar. "There's this absolutely adorable riverside condo in Elbow Park. It's perfect. But it won't last more'n a couple days."

Susan held her breath, counted to ten, exhaled slowly. Yasmina looked down at her hands.

"Mom? Are you there?"

"Your father would be beside himself if he heard you talk like this, Lauren. Please."

"Dad's been dead for three years now. I keep telling you."

"Do you really think I could forget that?"

Silence. Then Lauren's whisper. "Sorry, Mom."

"I know, honey. It's all right." Susan steadied herself. "Let's talk later. Promise." She gently set down the phone. "I'll get your clothes," she said to Yasmina. "To check their fit."

That evening, Susan sat cross-legged on the couch, doggedly picking stitches from the fragile tissue of the kameez. She'd misjudged the belling curve of the arms, and the act of reparation felt like a penance. The walls closed in. Maybe she'd been too hard on Lauren. Maybe she should sell the house. Maybe —

The doorbell rang. At the unexpected noise, the stitch ripper jabbed Susan's thumb. She dropped the fabric in a welter of jade and emerald, stuck her bleeding thumb in her mouth, left a smear of blood on the doorjamb.

"Yasmina!"

"I am so sorry to intrude."

"No, not at all! Come in."

"I cannot stay. I wished to bring you these." She held out a DVD case and a round stainless steel tin.

Susan felt tears well up as she regarded the packages. Peter had delighted in surprises.

"Oh, Susan. Do not cry. I just thought to give you a movie, my daughter's favourite when she was younger. *Bend it Like Beckham.* A bit of laughter, about football, with some curry and two girls. Like our daughters. Perhaps you've seen it already?"

Susan wiped her eyes. "That's so sweet of you. I've been watching the same dozen movies over and over again. Since Peter died."

"We'll talk about food instead. That is always a cheerful subject. Here." She thrust the tin toward Susan. "Hold it upright, like so, when you open it."

Susan balanced it on her lap and pried off the lid. Small tins nestled inside, filled with powders and seeds in shades of taupe, tan, ecru, cream, crimson. In the centre, seedpods the colour of new hay, pink and green peppercorns, amber kernels, dried rose petals.

"This is called *masala dhaba*."

"It's gorgeous!" Susan lifted the tin to her face and sniffed. Cinnamon she knew, and cloves. The rest blurred together in a sea of musk and woodsy pungency and bitterness and unsuspected pleasure. "What's it for?"

"Spices necessary for making curries. This is fennel, this is cumin. Cayenne. Mustard seeds. Roasted coriander. Turmeric. And this is our family's special blend I learned from my grandmother when I was very young. Fifteen spices. It is delicious with biryani."

"This is extraordinary. I've never been given anything like it."

"I will teach you. Yes?"

"Oh yes!"

"Lauren, what was that Woody Allen movie?" Susan cradled the phone on her shoulder and picked up the empty DVD case, the disc still in the player. The cover photograph — two teenaged girls in soccer jerseys, hugging — was as cheerful as the movie had been.

"Which one?"

"The one with that hilarious lobster scene."

"*Annie Hall*. Hey, do you remember when you tried to cook lobsters? Wasn't it Dad who finally picked them up out of the sink and dumped them in the pot head-first?" Lauren's giggle sounded like a child's.

How long had it been since she last laughed? Susan's body felt creaky. She breathed in, tentatively stretching, her lungs, her legs. "Your dad loved shellfish. I miss him so much."

"I miss him too, Mom."

"I know, honey." Susan stopped and re-ordered her thoughts. "Well, I was cutting down an *Annie Hall*–style jacket when this new client came to the door. I've drafted a new outfit for her."

"Wow, that's great! I don't know when you last designed something. That's partly why you should move. You could start a new business here. Generate a little income to boost Dad's pension and life insurance."

Trust Lauren to cut to the chase. "Well, don't worry," Susan said. "I want to tell you about this new client. She's brave. Funny."

"I'm glad you're finally meeting people. But let's get back to the possibility of you moving."

Susan gathered herself together, remembering the tin of spices Yasmina had brought her, trying to recall their names.

Cloves. Cumin. Coriander. Cinnamon. Fennel. And turmeric.

"Lauren, I don't want to get folded into a tiny corner of your life, and have you and Merrill resent me."

"I'd never resent you, Mom."

"You think that now, but if I was there and you were all I had, you would. I need to be here."

"But, Mom, what'll you do?"

"I've got my business. No more alterations — I want to see what other interesting clothing I can design. My garden needs attention. And I've made a friend. I told you, Yasmina, her name is. She likes movies. Maybe I can teach her to play cribbage. I'll take a trip to Calgary for fabric after I get some cash flowing." She stopped, breathless. A little dizzy.

"Mom — "

Susan could imagine her daughter's hand absently scrunching her wispy blonde hair into a ball on the top of her head. She'd been doing that since childhood. "What? What's wrong?"

"Nothing. Never mind. Are you sure?"

"I haven't been sure of anything for years, honey, and I'm not sure of this."

"Call me tomorrow, okay? Love you, Mom."

"I love you too. Come visit soon? I'll cook you some curry."

"Curry? You don't know how to make curry."

"I'm going to learn. Bye."

Susan dropped the phone and went into the bedroom. She swung the closet doors open, pulled out a flared yellow skirt embellished with poppies and vines, eyed it thoughtfully, flung it on the bed. Next was a sombre brown dress of crinkled linen, followed by a fitted black velveteen skirt and jacket — lovely fabrics, both, but the styles did no justice to her slipping belly. Nothing that suited her as she was now. She thought again of Yasmina, in her new suit when Susan had handed it over earlier that day, completely at ease in its ebb and flow of green and mauve.

Peter's smoking jacket hung alone on the top rack. She slid her arms into its sleeves and wrapped the jacket close. It still smelled of his aftershave.

Peter would urge her on, as he always had. She'd ask Yasmina to go shopping with her. For silk.

Fallen Sparrow

THE PLUM TREES HAVE JUST COME into bloom, and I'm standing behind my cart admiring their rosy canopy when the pain hits, a rocket blowing up in my ribcage, shooting deeper, into my lungs, as if one of my own kitchen knives is fracturing, shards of metal beneath my ribs. Gasp, bent double. Wheeze. Unable to draw a breath. Lurch to the park bench like some old rubby. Sit down, displacing the chickadees.

Slowly the pain recedes. When my eyes clear, I can see the birds again, their glittering black eyes beneath little monks' hoods, their voices flittering and purling. I'm still panting, light-headed, when a skinny teenager in torn jeans sashays up to me, about my height, his head cocked to one side, fair-skinned, bright bird-like eyes, a guitar on a fraying red cord slung over one shoulder. "I'm hungry," he says, holds out empty hands.

He's not the first homeless boy to ask me for food. I get up right away, stumbling a little, one hand clutching the back of the bench, the other on the rail of my cart, trying to conceal my frailties from this perfect child. As I fill a bun with bratwurst, I puzzle briefly over which condiments to include, settle for a gherkin, lace the bun with garlicky fried onions, dither between

Dijon or spicy malt mustard, my hand shaking as I reach across the cart to put the bun into his hands. "No charge."

The boy skips around to my side of the cart, smiles and plants a kiss on one cheek, then the other. As he saunters away among the pink blossoms, his voice trailing off like an unfinished melody, *"Merci beaucoup, ma tante,"* I completely forget about my chest. I don't have a Mother Superior to go to, so I go straight to the Mother, how I think of God, really. Old Soeur Jeanne-Marie always said that women hold up the sky, and from what I've seen in the world, she was right. How could God not be the Great Feminine, the Mother of All? I still believe, but I no longer wait for Her to solve my problems, I haven't since I left the convent. So I pray to Her. *Is this the child I never had, Mother?* I don't get an answer. Didn't expect to. I just hope the boy will come back. The hot knife-edge pains, I ignore again, as I have over the years. For weeks and months to come, in my private daily conversations with Her, a jaunty black-eyed boy will feature prominently and unexpectedly. I've learned that love cuts as deeply as those other invisible blades.

I arrived at the convent's orphanage in North Vancouver as a baby, sang French nursery rhymes, then Piaf and Aznavour's love songs, with Soeur Jeanne-Marie, learned long division from Sister Agnes. The convent bell's ringing amplified how much I longed to know my own mother; the nuns told me nothing of her. When I finally joined the order at twenty-five, the sole regret I attached to the order's requirement of chastity was that I would never have a child, a family of my own. Even obedience, if I could have kept my mind attentive, seemed no great struggle.

Not many women take the veil these days, so those who do fill many roles — I was both apprentice cook and gardener. Daydreaming in the garden instead of weeding, I would look up to find Sister Francesca standing in front of me, pointing at my basket and rasping, "Have you washed those greens yet, sister? Work is waiting."

Francesca was a Reuben-esque woman, as generous to me as God had been to her, with the biceps of a weight-lifter, thick white hair and sun-reddened skin, a hooked nose, the long blue gaze of patience. She was a German butcher's daughter, must have been stunning as a young woman, and passed her family's secrets on to me — my sausages for the cart are made as she taught me, with freshly ground pork, salt, maple syrup, chopped herbs and peppercorns, garlic, stuffed into pork casings and smoked over apple wood. When my knife slipped or I threw trimmings into the trash, she just smiled and patted me. "Well, young sister," she'd say in her stone-edged voice, and she'd wipe her butcher knife on the cloth at her hip, rescue the meat, wash it before grinding it. "Now you know better. From little, much can be made." Francesca and I fed the nuns, but also the convent's guests; they were few and far between, though, and loneliness walked with me in the garden.

"Did you ever want to have a child?" I asked one muggy summer day as we trimmed a pork shoulder, sweat sticking to my skin and making the knife handle into a weapon as I snipped and hacked at the meat beneath our hands.

"Gently, sister," she said. The knife she held wavered. "I raised my younger brother Andreas." I hesitated, reluctant to ask if there was an elder brother or sister, but she resumed speaking. "He is not like me. At all. Now, to your knife, sister."

"I want a family," I blurted. Beyond the aging sisters, I meant; beyond even Francesca. The hush of the kitchen's walls and the garden's fences chafed, and I jumped when the bell tolled in the tower, the notes rolling out, past the walls. "Don't you want to know the world? See the faces of the people you feed?"

Francesca just shrugged her heavy face skyward. "Pray."

I was young. Arrogant. I didn't pray so much as issue orders. *Show me how to have a family, Mother, I want to see lives changed by You!* Nothing changed, no burning bush, no mighty reverberating voice or even a renewed whisper in the moonlight. No orphaned children appeared, requiring succour. No mysterious partner-to-be knocked on the convent door, offering to father my children. I knew better, I decided, and I left two months after my thirty-third birthday. I went penniless. Nuns swear to poverty along with the other vows. Poverty seemed no great sacrifice. But Francesca sent me to her younger brother in Vancouver. "Andreas will help you," she said, a small hook in her voice. "He is a businessman, a 'venture capitalist', he tells me, so expect to pay for his help."

Andreas looked the polar opposite of his sister. Fine-boned and dapper. Silk scarf and a trilby hat on silver hair, a jaunty set to it. On the rack beside the kitchen door, a row of colourful jackets. A guitar leaned against the dining room wall. Piaf's voice, familiar since my childhood, on the stereo. *"Je ne regrette rien . . ."*

Somewhere inside his bright ground-floor apartment, a door slammed.

"Sister. One moment." He disappeared and I heard low voices, just a murmur. I peered over my shoulder as Andreas shepherded me out, a large wicker basket in his hand blocking my view of the door closing. Through the patio door, I saw the silhouette of a clean-cut head.

"So good of you to meet me here at home, the office is too far from the waterfront," he said cheerfully. "To the beach!" We ambled to nearby English Bay, and Andreas offered me dark-roast coffee from a thermos in his basket. Of course he already knew that Francesca had taught me the family trade. "Indeed, sister," he said, "I have some protégées, mostly younger than you, I suspect. One is an extraordinary baker, you must meet her. Here, try this," he said, proffering *pain au chocolat* in a meticu-lously pressed linen napkin. "So. An outdoor cart, Francesca suggests. Or perhaps a café?" Aghast, I shook my head. "Indeed, you may be right, a café is too much, even for a healthy woman in her — what? — thirties?" He pursed his lips and eyed my hands and wrists, still tanned from the convent garden. His mouth made a small moue, approval or disdain, I couldn't tell which. "Perhaps as Francesca suggests, an outdoor investment this time. Not a food truck, no, no, we want something petite, something charming, sufficient unto the needs of one small former nun. What about a little vending cart on wheels with wrought iron trim and maybe a roll-up canvas awning?" He paused. "Yes, just the thing, sister. Do you wish that we paint your given name on the awning?"

"Abigail? No one calls me that," I said, my mouth full of pastry. He would carry on calling me Sister for years. "Our Sister of the sausages," he would say, and ultimately, his joke became the fact, "Sister's Sausages" recorded on the cart's awning in flowing script.

Shock was settling into my body, numbing my hands, silencing me. Francesca had suggested that Andreas would help me, but I hadn't imagined how, thinking vaguely of a secretarial job, maybe a position in a church outreach ministry. Even as I drank his espresso and ate his croissants, it didn't occur to me that finding me a role in a church would never cross Andreas' mind, just as the possibility of having my own business would never enter mine. But so it was to be.

Andreas briskly patted my arm. "A deal, yes, sister?" All I could do was nod. "I will charge you some small strictly nominal interest," he went on. "Perhaps redeem a favour or two when I need sausages for my dinner parties. And here, my little welcome gift." He pulled a stainless steel espresso pot from the basket and held it out. "Do you have any family in Vancouver?"

I shook my head. "All dead. Just Francesca."

"So. We are family now."

That's how I became a street hawker. Francesca sent me her old meat grinder, the extra she kept under her bed just in case. Andreas found me a ground-floor furnished suite in subsidized housing near Main Street, with, wonder of wonders, a tiny gated yard.

"I had to pull a few strings," he said as we walked through the suite a week later. "And I will pay your rent until you establish yourself." He added more numbers to the tidy column beside my name in the little red book he carried in his jacket pocket.

"I may never be able to pay you back," I said dubiously. The apartment alone, even on the east side, never mind the red cart and awning, cost more money than I had ever anticipated having during my convent life.

"Not to worry, sister. I will take care of you, as Francesca asked. I had a good year, indeed I did. A healthy tax write-off keeps me good with my sister, and with her God. Keep your receipts. Now tell me, do you enjoy baseball? No, I supposed not. Ah well."

The city made me get a licence, and more numbers went into the red book.

"Research!" Andreas said, and handed me cash. I found a butcher with good pork, made test sausages, and invited my benefactor over to sample half a dozen varieties, ultimately settling on his sister's traditional bratwurst and my own ale and onion links.

After my cart became established on Cambie Street, in the lea of City Hall, beside a tiny park, he came by regularly, with an attractive young woman or youth on his arm, rarely the same person from one week to the next. Protégées, he said, never claiming any as his lover. On the summer day he introduced Elise and her sister, Patrice, both pale and narrow-hipped, I remembered the *pain au chocolat* I had tasted at our first meeting, and commissioned Elise on the spot. Handmade crusty rolls fit for my handmade sausages.

The neighbourhood cats and characters adopted me. I could see the cascade of buildings down the slope toward False Creek, and The Lions cut out against the sky to the north when the clouds cleared. I fed the same customers each week, frequently when the weather was fine, less so when the sky was cranky with rain. When the city expanded the transit line, and the new SkyTrain stop was added, my business leaped forward, and I saw how my small good daily works of smoked sausages made my customers smile. But there was never a special smile for me. I was always lonely. Sundays, I spent my afternoons at the community kitchen, making soup for the homeless women and their hungry children who crowded in, looking for beds and reassurances. The women, their faces aging beyond their years, needed the Mother even more than I did. Everywhere I looked, want and hunger were ahead of me. To even consider spending time searching for a special friend was out of the question in the face of such need; a woman like me could fill her days cooking, feeding, and the hunger would never be fed.

I had mornings to myself as I packed my coolers with sausages and condiments, humming to Verdi, records I found at the thrift shop for pennies, and a vintage record player too. One day in my kitchen, some weeks after I had met the black-eyed boy, I bent over the mortar and pestle, garlic and nutmeg fragrant in my nose while my espresso pot burbled and spat. In its curved silver face I saw my reflection pull into a jester's grimace as knives plunged into my chest. I buckled to the floor, my chest compressing, heard the pot tumble, the gush of liquid against the tiles, Rigoletto caught in the skipping grooves.

Andreas found me an hour later on his daily coffee-klatsch swing through the neighbourhood. His companion stood in the background, a sleek young man in brown silk, eying my open cupboards with a scarcely hidden sneer while Andreas fussed.

"Sister! Such a terrible thing!" he said, kneeling beside me and gesturing at the silk suit to lift the needle off the record. "An embolism, perhaps. Or your heart. This is serious. We must get you to the clinic. My nephew will call an ambulance."

I demurred, befuddled by the image of Andreas with a mop in his hands, tidying my kitchen floor, and the pains eased soon enough. It took a day or two before his choice of noun came back to me: "nephew." Andreas had one sister, and she was childless. But my confusion faded along with the pain, and it didn't matter.

My recurrent pain is far from my thoughts on a cloudy summer afternoon. A few months have passed since the unknown boy begged a sausage from me, and I've run out of maple syrup and garlic. So I take the bus to the market beneath the Granville Street bridge. Walking back, stopping in at Elise's bakery, fragrant with yeast and sugar and chocolate, perched beside the cobbled path along False Creek, I hand Elise a cooler packed with bratwurst. She looks white and thin, skin etched with the charcoal of fatigue.

"How is Patrice?" I ask. "How is her appetite? Shall I bring weisswurst for her next week? They are mild."

She wraps half a dozen *pain au chocolat* in parchment, shrugging as she ties a string around the package and passes it to me. "Patrice can't eat anything after chemo, sister. And Andreas wants me to expand. He says it's time for us to make some real money on his investment. I can't. It takes all my energy just to care for Patrice. She'll be in a hospice soon enough. But the idea of managing more staff makes me cringe. I can't possibly. Not now." She rubs her hands on her face, leaves a smear of flour under her shadowed eyes. "I owe Andreas everything, but you know what he's like. I feel so guilty at the idea of saying no. Nothing to do with you, sister. Sorry to burden you." She gives me another packet. "Here. For the birds."

As I walk along the seawall, I'm thinking of Elise and her dilemma, caught on the rocks of a dying sister and business obligation. And Andreas, oh yes, I do indeed know what he's like. It's taking me years to repay his loan, although to his credit, he never chastises me for missing the odd month. Throwing bits of stale bread to the shrieking gulls, I ruminate about the open hands of those forces that surround others: parents, business partners, siblings. Children. I've been out in the world for a decade, and beyond the small needs of my cart, I still have few ties to bind me. I feel the lack keenly.

Watching the arc of birds across the sky, I trip on an uneven cobble. My ankle twists beneath me, and I tumble to my hands and knees, land in a puddle, my pastry and groceries askew across the path. So here I am, scrambling around, relieved the maple syrup is still intact in its glass jar, gathering up the garlic, my nose inches from the stones, mildly cursing the birds and my own inattention, when I hear a voice.

"Help you?"

I look up to see the lovely black-eyed boy of the park. Of the surprise kiss. He grins and holds out one hand, helps me up and eyes my pastries while I shove everything back onto my tote, but I don't argue when he pulls the bag from my hands, the sting in my ankle shouting for ice. My groceries knock against the battered guitar on his hip all the way back to my suite, and when I try to thank him, that wide white smile blooms. As he leaves, I give him two croissants.

He finds me at the cart again the next day. He's fifteen, looks twelve, nobody to love, a street kid with a Québécois accent. Sylvain. Around massive bites of bratwurst, he tells me about his lost *Maman*. As I listen, I send a prayer into the ether, a wordless thank-you to her and to the Mother. For his sake, and for mine.

"She was a yoga teacher, eh, and when we get Vancouver we were broke. She leave me with her girlfriend, for just the evening, *t'sais*, and she go to the park. Not this *petit*." He waves an expansive hand at the park we sit in. "The big one by the water."

"Stanley Park?"

"*Oui.*"

"Had she left you alone before? To go to the park?"

His face closes. "Maybe. This time, she die. Stabbed, hmmm. And now I am just me alone. I keep away from La Welfare, they want to put me with some strangers." He's surprisingly sanguine. Somehow he has learned to trust in the universe, and he is still whole, still safe. The Mother is watching this French sparrow.

I watch over him too, he's raggedly thin. He visits me just before I close up every afternoon, always hungry, with a motley entourage of boys in tattered jeans and outgrown runners. I feed them, all the sausages they want, even though each bite means less cash towards paying back Andreas. The boys enjoy my company, and after they finish eating they lounge on the cement planters and stairs that flank the street, Sylvain perched close to my cart. We feed the birds and he tells me about his mother's meetings with famous movie-star yoga devotees, then he plays his guitar and sings, his high voice rippling melodies into the clouds.

I don't know where Sylvain sleeps. Prying goes against the privacy I learned in the convent, but a beautiful boy like him must take risks to survive. I am afraid to ask. I don't want to know. I start bringing extra croissants, apples and yoghurt with me, and it isn't long before he puts on a few pounds, and soon he's left the street lads behind and is sleeping on the couch in the living room. Then I teach him how to make sausage. He's curious, with quick fingers and a nimble mind, and he especially loves the smoker I have bolted onto the fence around my yard, a hinged metal box contrived with parts Andreas' handyman found for me. Sylvain likes to feed applewood into the firebox and smell the sweet smoke when the fire slows, links of sausages dangling above the coals. It reminds him of the sugaring-off at home, he says, the fire and the buckets of maple sap, the thickened syrup congealing.

Before the summer winds to a close, I have him smoking sausages on Fridays, selling at the cart with me on Saturdays.

All this long wet autumn, on my weekly visits to Francesca, I take him with me on the SeaBus across the harbour to North Vancouver. Francesca, who has risen to Mother Superior in the convent, smiles at him as he fidgets in the chapel, nods over his head at me, and sends us back across the water with bags bulging, heaped full of chard, wild mushrooms, arugula, onions, beets.

"Do you see my brother often?" she inquires one afternoon as we step into the late October gale. "Does he still love baseball? Is he still alone?"

"Oh, I see Andreas every week, for coffee. He's fine." I'm so happy to show off my boy that I forget to mention Andreas' "nephew," and it slips my mind until we get home. Sociable Andreas, never alone. I forget about her query.

It's clear that Sylvain doesn't like Andreas when they meet. I've told Andreas about my new family member, and he arrives with a gift in hand, a black and gold baseball jacket, eyes Sylvain closely as he holds it out to him. Sylvain puts his hands behind his back, and Andreas drapes the jacket on a chair.

"Looks like it should fit," he says, his nasal voice flat and non-committal. "Perhaps your new friend would like to come to watch the ballgame in the park with me some evening next spring when the season gets going, sister? I always have an extra ticket. What say you, Sylvain? Have you seen the city's baseball team, the Canadians, play at Nat Bailey Stadium?" When Sylvain doesn't respond, Andreas looks at me, shrugs and carries on. "Ever hear of José Canseco? A hell of a hitter. He was a Canadian, once upon a time."

Sylvain shakes his head, his lips pursing in a way I haven't seen before.

Andreas kisses my cheeks as usual before he leaves. "A surly lad," he whispers. "D'you trust him?" He seems unconvinced when I nod.

But Sylvain is not to be bought so easily. "Eh, *il est un poppy fleuri*, like those men, *Maman's patrons*," he says grimly as Andreas closes the gate behind him and strolls down the street. It's his first admission of his mother's true income source, of her meetings, not with movie stars or yoga enthusiasts, but with clients of a different sort. After a few days, he tires of moving the jacket from chair to kitchen counter to chair, and finally, he tries it on, then parades in the narrow hallway, the irony completely lost on him. "Hmmm, what you think, *ma tante?* Why he bring me gifts?"

I consider. The unexplained nephew. Andreas would have no interest in Sylvain. He's just a child. But still I avoid giving Sylvain a straight answer, and take the easy road. "Sylvain, he's generous. He's been my friend for a long time."

Sylvain looks at the jacket and wrinkles his nose. A few days later, he begins to wear it, and has it on one afternoon when Andreas stops by with freshly roasted coffee beans.

"Sylvain," I urge, "say thank you to Andreas."

Sylvain's black eyes appraise Andreas, a frank sweeping study, then slide away.

In the mornings, over *café au lait* and *pain au chocolat*, I harangue him. "Trade school, Sylvain. Maybe music classes, hmm? Or baking? Learning to make good pastry like Elise? You can't be on the street all your life." *Street life will kill you.* I can't bring myself to say it. "You could learn from Elise. Her new shop needs apprentice bakers, now that Patrice has died." I almost have him there: croissants from her new location farther up Cambie Street are a morning staple that Sylvain looks forward to.

"Why I learn to bake? I have you. And you have Elise. Perfect. No school. I make the sausages for you, and music." He brushes his hands clean of crumbs and picks up his guitar. "À bientôt, ma tante."

No trade school. No job with Elise. The day he comes home with a new black hoodie, he stubbornly turns his face away from me and will not say how he came by it.

"Did you steal this, Sylvain? We do not steal!"

"No, ma tante." His face is impassive. He refuses to say anything else. Finally, frustrated, I drop the matter. A few days later, it's a new shirt. Then expensive jeans. Each time he walks in with new clothing, he evades my eyes, but will admit nothing. "I am no thief," is all he says.

He teaches me a few French words, but I stop using them when I realize, after a few horrified glares from francophone customers, that they're gutter slang. Weekdays at my cart, I listen for his voice and his guitar drifting from the far end of the park where he busks, singing in French and then English. But some evenings, he comes in late, falling onto the couch without his customary "Good night, ma tante."

Those nights, I'm plagued by chest pains and fear. I lie without moving in my narrow bed, watching the shadows advance across the thin draperies. I try to pray, but the Mother seems a world removed. In the morning light, my cheeks in the mirror are wan. Sylvain sleeps late and wakes sluggish and irritable, his face stretched and thin, scowling at me as I pack my cooler for the noon rush of park-side walkers. I catch the whiff of scent on his skin when I hug him, and I wonder. But I don't have the heart to confront him.

I spot him one day, across the street from my cart one afternoon, heading to the SkyTrain with another youth. Both are lustrous otters, Sylvain in a silver-studded t-shirt and tailored pants I don't recognize. I call and wave, and both heads swivel toward me, then quickly away.

I know they see me.

The slight cuts worse than any knife. When he comes in to sleep, I don't leave my bed to enquire where they went. I don't know how to ask, and I don't want to know.

His face is changing, its narrow hawkish cast becoming more pronounced and secretive. Life as a nun and a park-side vendor has not prepared me for tough-love parenting. The next day after lunch winds down, I take the SeaBus by myself, across the choppy inlet to see Francesca.

"Do you have a nephew?" I ask as soon as I enter her office where she is bent over paperwork. She rarely works in the kitchen anymore.

"No, of course not," she says in surprise.

"A son?"

"No! You know that. I am as you see me. Come outside, to the garden, sister. You have something on your mind beyond Sylvain?"

"Yes, and no," I say.

We drink our tea, tidying the raised beds in their wooden frames as we speak.

"Sylvain has money. Clothes. I think he's having sex. For pay. With strangers," I say, and I'm surprised, both at my bluntness and at how easily the words come to me.

"Ah. I suspected that might happen," Francesca says. "Children sometimes go wrong no matter what their families do, sister. We all have our own karma."

I look at her in surprise. My friend has never spoken like this before.

"He wouldn't come along today?" she asks.

"I didn't ask."

"Maybe I should ask Andreas to have a word? No? Leave it to me, then. Make sure Sylvain is at your cart on Friday." She pulls a few late onions, brushes off the soil. "Here. Put these in your tote bag." She sends me home with a benediction, but the calm is torn out of me by the wind as I board the SeaBus.

I hardly lay down my head at night all week, waiting. I can't talk to Her, and Sylvain is rarely around. When he appears, he wears a shell as impervious as my raingear. "Yes, *ma tante*," he says to any question I ask, his voice mechanical and rigidly polite. I want to shake him, ask, where is the lovely boy I adore?

On Friday, the autumn wind chases up the slope from False Creek. Over breakfast, as Francesca has suggested, I ask Sylvain to meet me at the cart after lunch. "The awning is sticking in the wind," I say, "I can't reach the ratchet to roll it down." He nods, looking down at the table, aligning croissant crumbs with his fingertip. His fingers are smooth, their nails immaculately shaped.

At noon, Francesca meets me at the cart. I sit her down on the bench out of the breeze and hand her lunch. An hour later, then two hours, and the day's customers are long gone, with no sign of Sylvain.

Francesca is tight-lipped. "So sorry, my dear," she says, hugging me. "I thought this might be how it would go. He is leaving you slowly. Best to be ready." My chest feels perforated, my breath leaking out.

No sign of him at home. Guitar, his fancy clothes, gone. Just a note, scrawled and cocked against a water glass on the kitchen table. "Bye-bye, *ma tante*."

I stand in the echoing kitchen, crying. Then I rage, peppering Her with my anger. *Why did he have to go? You are no true Mother!*

I post signs, offer a reward. I even go to the police. But they just shrug. Another street kid, I can see it in their faces. Finally I mourn, sit in my apartment drinking espresso, listening to my sad Verdi. My sparrow has flown.

Andreas loses patience, and becomes territorial about his apartment after I spot a gold-trimmed black jacket hanging among his scarves on one of my visits.

"Is that . . . ?" I almost run from room to room, banging doors open.

Andreas hesitates, then catches himself, and me, as I pass him. "What? You mean Sylvain's? Of course it is, you know he's been here half a dozen times with you! But I haven't seen that ungrateful boy since he left you high and dry. He just forgot it here. Calm down, sister."

Several weeks later, he meets me at the door. "Let's go down the street for coffee. A new cleaning lady," he says smoothly. "She is such a tyrant, she swears she can smell garlic after you have been here." I sniff, insulted, and stop dropping by unannounced.

I owe Andreas and Francesca more than loyalty. But faced with what feels like his waning friendship and the risk of expulsion from his family circle, I retreat. Long days creep by, the rainy season endured as I drink my bitter coffee alone at Elise's new bakery. She commiserates, but has no time to talk. If I didn't still owe money to Andreas, I'd sell the cart and leave the park, but I refuse to return to the convent. I have nowhere to go.

Life carries on. I make sausages, sell them. The plum and cherry trees bloom, then turn green. A year passes. My grief dulls. I see Andreas every month, but only when he comes by my apartment to collect my payment, his voice formal. I turn back to the Mother, and visit Francesca whenever I can, feeling as grey as the water of Burrard Inlet splashing across the bow of the ferry. The sound of my whining heart dismays me, but I can't set it aside.

Francesca is less brusque than I expect. "There is no schedule for pain, or for healing," she says one bleak afternoon, her hands gentle on mine. "The therapists say, a year for this loss, six months for that one, but we heal when we are ready to heal, sister." She holds out a bag, fronds of fresh dill weed peeking out from the top. "Are you eating? Here are new potatoes and herbs. And don't fret so about Andreas. He is worried about you. He simply has small patience with suffering. Don't make the mistake of thinking that he doesn't care for you."

I adopt the habit of staying late at the cart, unwilling to go home to my empty suite, preferring to watch the summer sky, the birds, the late stragglers walking out of downtown. One bright evening, I am surprised to see Andreas, resplendent in a plaid linen jacket, complete with trilby, striding toward my cart.

"Hello, sister."

"Alone tonight, Andreas?"

"Hopeful of your company, sister. I've been remiss in attending to my business interests. My apologies. Your chest, any pain lately? None? Good. Very good. Pack up quickly, and I'll take you to the ball game." He holds up a pair of tickets.

I feel a twinge at being relegated to "business interests." But I've never been to a ball game and the Mother advocates faith, and gratitude: he's my benefactor, and Francesca's brother.

Whistling, he perches on the bench as I pack the sausages into my cooler and lock the storage cupboard on the bottom of the cart, crank the umbrella to rest, and wrestle with the chain, tangled in the wheels of the cart, until my chest begins to throb. I stop, drew a breath, and wait for it to fade, my back turned to Andreas.

We take a cab to the stadium. Andreas hands me into the bleachers and goes off for pretzels. I'm content to sit in the sun. The field glitters like emeralds, the pure white of the lines etched in a diamond around the grass. The players, long shadows in the evening light, are joking and laughing, playing, and glad of it.

"What's he doing?" I ask when Andreas returns, pointing at a youngster dragging a sack onto the field.

"He's the batboy. See, he's hauling out all the baseball bats for the hitters to choose from."

Immersed in watching the batboy, my heart rises and falls. When I first spotted him, I'd thought for a half-breath that it was Sylvain. But that's impossible; this is a child, fair-haired, younger than Sylvain had been when we met. He has the same deft way of going that Sylvain had, though, as if he's leaping for the moon. Same grin, I see him break it out only once, a wide beam as light as his feet, when the first batter comes over to him and collects a bat. The first pitch.

As the innings unwind, I watch effortless catches and mighty strikes and the irresistible game of stealing bases, my eyes going back to the boy. Longing fills my mouth. *Mother, wherever he is, keep my boy safe.*

At the top of the fifth inning, Andreas flags down a vendor and buys me a beer and a hotdog. "My treat, sister. Forget you are the sausage queen and try this." Sitting in the late evening sunlight, I want things to be other than they are. I want the cheap hot dog to taste like my bratwurst, and the watery lager to remind me of Francesca's youthful Munich pilsner. Most of all, I want Sylvain, and things to be as they had been. Tears dribble down my cheeks.

Andreas notices, and gently puts a folded cotton handkerchief into my hand without fuss.

When the game winds into the final inning, he nudges me. "You know you can go right down to the field and say hi to the ball players. I bet some of them have bought sausages from you."

Too big a group of strangers to face alone. But the thought of a closer look at the boy is irresistible. After the final pitch, I carefully make my way down the steps. The sun is going down and I have the last rays in my eyes as I step down each riser, my sight set on the field. Four steps from the bottom, I see the batboy, in his hand a ball hypnotically tossed up and down, like a falling and rising charm.

My chest feels flayed open, the knife again, through my ribs. I topple down the remaining steps, pain arcing into my shoulder and arm. From the corner of my eye I see the boy, standing by the players' bench a few strides from the seats at the foot of the staircase, his face turning to me in slow motion as I tumble to his feet.

I open my eyes and find myself under a blanket on an ambulance stretcher, staring into a pair of brown eyes behind wire glasses, their owner kneeling beside my hip, a clipboard in his fingers. Andreas stands beside him, hands clasped behind his back, his face anxious. At his shoulder, I can see another slim figure. I want the unknown one to take that half step forward into my life, but he stands immobile.

The paramedic's voice draws me back. "Ma'am? Do you have a history of stroke? Heart disease? Embolism?"

"Maybe." My voice like a raven's. More knives. My eyes fly past the medic's cap, trying to focus on the sparrow-like figure behind Andreas.

"I'm going to start you on blood thinners. Okay?" I nod carefully. It hurts to breathe or move.

The batboy finally steps into view and speaks, an unfamiliar soprano. "You gonna be all right, lady?"

I try to move my head, and I can't help myself, I begin to weep, dry sobs that tear at my chest, more of relief than suffering. Sylvain, his quick smile, his charm, such a miracle. He's not coming back, my boy. But this boy's innocent face tells me of the many other children in the world. I've loved once; I might again find a child who needs to be loved.

"You know each other?" The paramedic's voice is gentle.

Andreas intercepts the medic's query. "She is my sister." He looks down at me. His eyes are as blue as Francesca's. "And this time, it is to the hospital. I will come, and I will call Francesca. Haven't I always taken care of you? We are family."

He lays his hand on my wrist. Comforting me, I know, as I contemplate all the answers I want to give.

Exercise Girls

I WAS FIFTEEN WHEN I TRESPASSED up the long driveway to visit the horses grazing behind the fence. I'd studied those horses all spring while walking the half-mile home from the bus stop with my little sister Jill. Thoroughbreds, I guessed, what I'd want to be if I were a horse, so elegant and spare — a far cry from my own compact frame, more like a Welsh pony. The horses reminded me of Dad.

Dad had called me his pit pony whenever I'd drop my head and plug away at homework I didn't quite get. "You don't quit, do you, Fanny?" he'd tease, stroking my unruly hair as if it was a mane in need of grooming. I missed him so much my bones ached, a dull intermittent pain. Forty years later I still miss him, and I wonder how that year would have played out if he'd been alive.

One horse, long-legged, a dainty head like an Arab's, perked his ears at me. I dropped to my knees beside the gate and was rummaging in my backpack when a man in faded Levis and denim jacket, tall and narrow as a hinge, strode from an adjacent field milling with Hereford cattle. He stood watching me from the far side of the gate. Beneath the tilt of his cowboy hat, his eyes were the brown of the slow-moving water in the nearby canal, and his hatchet face was creased like linen dried on the clothesline. Frayed cuffs left his wrists naked and I could see black hairs threading toward his knuckles. My breathing rasped unexpectedly and I could feel the skin of my throat get warm as I looked up at him. I had to look away, forty yards down the lane to where Jill was flipping the red flag up and down on the rusty mailbox at the driveway's end, shifting from one foot to the other. I mouthed warnings at her, then turned back to the lanky man in blue.

"No sugar," he said sharply as I pulled something from my pack. He half-smiled when he saw the carrots in my hand, lit a cigarette, talked around it. "That's fine, girlie."

The red horse stood aloof and wary, watching as I leaned over the barbed wire and held out the carrots, but the fine-boned bay approached me willingly. I was stretching out a cautious hand to stroke that black muzzle when the rough voice resumed.

"You grow up with horses?"

"My daddy was a rodeo bullfighter," I said, surprised when my voice didn't break. "He bought me a mare five years ago, she's part Arab. Meara." He looked blankly at me. "From *Lord of the Rings*," I added, uncomfortably aware I was blathering, but he didn't seem to notice.

"You got the hands."

I flushed and dropped a carrot, shoved the remaining one and my freckled hands with their gnawed nails out of sight. He didn't say anything else. But I felt his eyes until I reached Jill, took her hand and turned west. All I could smell were the possibilities of spring in the Fraser Valley, wet alfalfa's green funk, musky sedge leaking into early bloom, the old-socks rankness of cattails.

At home, we fed Meara the last carrot. I breathed in her sweet breath, feeling somehow guilty, but I couldn't put my finger on why. Meara had carried me on a loose rein in the long year since Dad died, my unquestioning friend in my struggles to fit into a new school and a new house. Mom had sold our Aldergrove home, its fields and big white barn, right after the funeral last spring. "We've got to cut expenses," she'd said curtly when Jill and I protested. "We need something smaller, closer to Chilliwack." She'd just started at the York canning plant, working the evening shift, and after I spent that summer taking care of Jill, I started to think about getting a summer job of my own, looking ahead to university. I couldn't do anything yet but take care of little kids and ride horses, but I didn't want a life like Mom's, her skin and body wearing away to nothing, overshadowed by the sickly-sweet scent of overcooked asparagus or peaches or corn that clung to her.

As we ate our macaroni and cheese, Jill startled me by announcing, "Fanny gave away her lunch today."

Mom, her face shadowed by the potted fig tree beside the dining room table, immediately looked awake. "Tired of egg salad, Fan? Your favourite."

"Carrots, not sandwiches," Jill said, her lisp making her words fuzzy. "She gave them to a big horse."

Mom sighed and picked at her lettuce. She'd shrunk since Dad's death. I'd given up trying to get her to wear anything other than baggy jeans and one of his grey plaid shirts buttoned over her camisole. At the recent parent-teacher interviews, I'd worried when I saw how dull her skin seemed beside my PhysEd teacher, who glowed in a flowing Indian cotton dress and scarf. But I couldn't get her to eat more. All she wanted was salad and mint tea.

Mom didn't ask questions, but I felt an unfamiliar hint of guilt, worried about what my sister might say next, careful to not mention the horses or their owner as Jill climbed into the bunk above me and we settled down to read. I went to sleep with my fingers flat across the tender skin of my belly, caressing the jut of my pelvic bone, and dreamed about the tall man with the narrow hands.

The next day, I sent Jill ahead of me when we got off the after-school bus. "I'll be right behind you," I said and shoved her gently homeward. "Just go have a snack. Soon as I'm home we'll read the next chapter of *The Red Pony*." Then I walked up the horseman's lane with the apple I'd saved from my lunch. I hovered at the gate, twisting the straps of my backpack until the man emerged from the barn.

"You again. You got no schoolwork to keep you out of trouble?" He snapped his fingers at the bay nosing my apple. "This here's Nero. What's your name, girlie?"

"Fanny."

"You want a job? I could use an exercise girl. Muck out the barn, clean tack, take the horses to the lake. Some gallops here on my track. Think you could handle that?" A searching look from beneath the brim of the cowboy hat. "Five bucks an hour. Call me Roy."

"I have to ask my mom," I said, my breath caught in my throat, and ran to catch up with Jill.

None of my classmates rode horses but I asked my cowboy-crazy best friend Sheila about Roy. She told me during biology class that she'd heard some gossip at the record store. He liked to hire girls. Had three kids. A wife who'd been his exercise rider back in the day. Her voice rose half a peg. "Why the interest?"

"Just a job," I hurried to say. There was nothing to admit, I told myself fiercely. Nothing. But I couldn't explain away the flutter of doves' wings in my chest.

"Boring," Sheila said. "He's so *old*!"

Inwardly, I modified her words. He was a man. Not a boy.

Sheila tugged her skirt up a little higher and turned the talk back to sex while she stared at our teacher as if he was a butterfly she wanted to pin, her back arched so her breasts pushed forward. I still felt acutely self-conscious about my own breasts and hid them under loose t-shirts, but Sheila wore hers proudly, like medals she had earned, their soft swellings edged with a lace bra clearly visible from the neckline of her peasant blouse. Waving a glass slide like a conductor's baton, she said, "Fanny, why don't you just let one of the boys kiss you and get it over with? Peter, maybe, he's always talking about you. Don't be such a priss. Everyone does it."

I turned my face to the microscope, blushing as she recounted her latest date at a recent concert, kisses and surreptitious touching, fumbling hands and mouths to the backbeat of steel guitars and cowboy tenors. But my body paid attention in a way it hadn't when Mom had coloured and stumbled over words during "our talk" several months before Dad's death. She'd brought home educational films from the library, both of us hemmed inside our chairs as we'd watched images too graphic to be mistaken for just another biology lesson. I couldn't meet her eyes when she turned off the VCR. How could I equate *that* with the stirrings I felt, with my electrified skin, the shivering fine hairs along my bare arms? But each time I witnessed Peter's red-faced embarrassment when I accidentally caught his eye at the bus stop, I dismissed him. A boy. His body thick, his face pocked. Graceless. I thought of the lithe horseman, and wished again that Dad was still alive, although I might have hidden this particular mystery from him. Now, I believe he'd have waded in with advice despite his discomfort. He'd been that kind of man, matter-of-factly brave beyond bulls.

The following Saturday morning, I leaned my bike against Roy's barn wall and spotted him through the kitchen window as he waved me into the house.

The house smelled of coffee, horses and babies. Roy eyed me. "You bring your helmet?" He nonchalantly arched his arm in my direction from his seat at the table. "My wife, Lisa. This is Fanny."

I looked into a pale face, wrinkles beginning to erode the skin around mouth and nose. A mane of uncombed black hair. Amber-flecked eyes, a mouth like a whip. She was an inch shorter than me, diaper-clad baby on one hip, half her face shuttered by the fall of her hair. A pair of brown-haired boys, about four years old, identical except for the colour of their t-shirts, romped on the floor at her feet, yelping and laughing.

Roy tipped an eyebrow toward the counter. "Want coffee? Help yourself."

Dad had been a coffee hound, but he'd refused to let me do more than sniff his morning mug. This was my first taste. It was unexpectedly bitter. I wasn't sure I liked it, but I sipped as I watched the boys wrestle. My bones felt too big for my body. In that hothouse of a room, I ached for my uncomplicated dad, his self-effacing shrug and half-sideways grin that showed his chipped tooth and smoothed the edges of everything he did.

Ten minutes felt like an hour by the time Roy stretched to his feet. I set down my half-full mug with relief, its thump echoing into the silence. Lisa stood wordlessly at the sink as I thanked her, her child wide-eyed on her hip. "It's Derby Day, Secretariat's running," Roy said to her, then whistled sharply at the twins. "Tell them boys to watch their cartoons early. I'll be in later to see the race." They stopped wrestling, looked up from the floor at him, then sideways in unison at Lisa. She stubbed out her cigarette, her face slamming shut as she studied me as closely as Roy had at the gate. I sniffed and picked up my crash helmet. What kind of woman would let herself get so dog-eared? But even as the thought floated through my brain, I could picture my mother's haggard face.

"You hear of Secretariat, girlie?" he asked as we walked to the barn.

I shook my head. I didn't know racehorses other than what I'd read in Dick Francis novels, although my bookshelf always overflowed, *National Velvet* leaning on *The Black Stallion*. *Black Beauty* beside *The Art of Horsemanship*, *A Leg at Each Corner* lying open at the first cartoon pony.

"You will. This is Alexander. Saddle up."

At the sight of the red stallion in the barn, I forgot what I'd been thinking. He didn't flinch when I tossed on the saddle, but he leaned obstinately away when I raised the bridle. "You're too short," Roy said, gestured toward an old wooden stepstool beside the wall. "Use that, it's hers. Lisa's."

I dragged the stool into the centre of the aisle, climbed up, slid the bit past long slanting teeth, smoothed the leather straps behind tufted ears. Outside, Roy gave me a leg up, then held the stirrup iron as I fumbled my boot into it. The exercise saddle felt absurdly small, nothing to really sit in, just a bit of leather to perch above.

"He likes to come out fast, but he don't go far," Roy said. "Just take him three furlongs."

I didn't get a chance to ask what a furlong was. Roy led the horse onto the narrow dirt track that followed the farm's fence-line, turned him loose and chirruped once. The long ears ahead of me flickered and Alexander erupted into a gallop. I grabbed what wisps of mane I could and steadied myself in the tiny saddle, my legs tucked up like a grasshopper's. I glanced down once. Beneath us, the black soil rushed past, so close. Those four flashing legs all that kept me safe. I raised my head, felt the wind whip my grin from my face and toss it behind us. A wince of guilt slid through me; even at her fastest, Meara was a slug compared to this horse.

He abruptly slowed into a shuffling trot, and I had my breath back by the time we stood in front of Roy. He pulled his cigarette out of his mouth and cocked his head to look up at me. "Not bad, girlie. Want the job?"

School finished. I promised Sheila I'd visit her in town, knew I wouldn't. She'd only want to debate how far to go with her string of impatient guitar-playing boys. Instead, my summer routine unfurled in stinging sweat, the warm muddle of leather, horses and box stalls, the growing tension in my body. Mom had acquiesced when I told her I'd found a job exercising racehorses. "Be home in time to mind Jill when my evening shift starts," she'd said, "and just be careful." I knew she didn't mean speed or protecting my teeth or eyes. I resolutely blocked out thoughts of

Dad. He might've liked Roy, but not as my new boss, although the job itself would have tickled his fancy.

Mornings, I joined Roy and Lisa in their sunny kitchen, Roy's feet in his dusty cowboy boots propped up on a chair, Lisa chain-smoking on the window bench, the baby and twins on the floor. "That Secretariat," he'd say, shaking his head, "Done it again. The Triple Crown last month, the Arlington Invitational last week. Never seen anything like it." After he drank two cups of coffee, the *Sun's* daily racing pages fallen to the floor beside the baby, Roy led me out to the barn.

Every day I watched Roy walk in and out of stalls, denim jeans taut across his narrow hips. I stopped biting my nails and stripped off my stained work gloves whenever I thought he would hand me a pitchfork or tub of saddle soap. My skin shivered as he ran his hands down his horses' legs. "Here, girlie," he'd beckon, then grab my hand, pulling me to my knees beside him where he squatted in the straw. His fingertips firm on my hands, guiding them down the horse's shin. "Feel that tendon along the cannon bone? Gotta watch it for heat or swelling." He dropped my hand and pushed himself to his feet. I gasped inside as he walked away.

Some days, I galloped Alexander or Nero around the rough track, Roy's cattle watching us stupidly from the next field. Other days, I took Nero to the Vedder canal and we waded in murky water that splashed up onto my boots. On the far bank, brambles hung, jungles of thorns and canes glittering with blackberries. Most days, I daydreamed about Roy, imagining something less tarnished than Sheila's casual experiments. I had to pull Nero to a halt before I rode back onto the yard, think about the muscles of my face, rearrange them into a mask while I cleaned the mud from his fetlocks and hooves.

I didn't call Sheila. I collapsed into my bed after late suppers, ignoring Jill, pretending to sleep so she wouldn't ask me to read or brush her hair. Roy and his horses galloped into my dreams and I woke each morning with shamefaced pleasure, anxious to see them again.

One morning in late July, Alexander was tied in his box stall when I arrived. "Two mares comin' over," Roy said over coffee. He looked at me inquiringly. "Ever see a stallion cover a mare?"

I blushed and shook my head, acutely conscious of Lisa. But when I looked up, she was gazing intently at her husband, not at me.

"Thought not," he said easily. "Too young. You'd best go home."

On a humid August evening after supper, I needed to get out. Jill was whining. "There's nothing to do. I'm hot."

I ignored her pouting as I saddled Meara. "There's ice cream in the freezer. You can watch *My Friend Flicka* again. And stay in the house!" I yelled as I left, guilt pricking at me for abandoning her despite Mom's specific instructions. Just an hour.

At Roy's, I tied up Meara, saddled Nero and urged him around the track, my mind flattening with every stride, then shepherded him into the pasture to graze. Roy ambled up and leaned against a dogwood tree, cigarette hanging loosely from his mouth. He tipped his cowboy hat back and watched as I tidied the saddle, running the belly-band between clanking stirrups, looping bridle reins, sponging away sweat stains. His hands toyed with a mane comb. Finally, when my skin was twitching from his silent inspection, he pulled his hat forward so most of his face was in shadow. "Trailerin' to Osoyoos races end of the month, Fanny. You comin'?"

"To groom or to ride?"

"Groom. Some things you still too young for, girlie. Not for much longer, though, eh?" His brown eyes narrowed, barely visible beneath his hat brim.

"I'll ask my mom," I said, but I knew what she'd say. I put the saddle away, swung onto Meara and kicked her into a canter. No wave for Lisa, invisible behind her kitchen window, but I felt Roy's eyes.

Instead of going home, I turned Meara along the canal's flat shoulder, hoping to ride my body into exhaustion. The valley's green shoulders were lush from the summer's rain. Cormorants were fishing in the shallow water, blackberries ripening, but even from Meara's back, I couldn't reach the best where they dangled, protected by spines of barbed wire and bramble.

Darkness had arrived by the time I unsaddled and brushed Meara. Jill was asleep on the couch, the television blaring. I picked her up and hauled her into bed.

The next morning, steamy unfallen rain hung over the valley, blocking sight of the hills. Jill, at the table eating dry cereal with her fingers, turned to me and sing-songed, "Fanny has a boyfriend, Fanny has a boyfriend!"

"Shush! You'll wake Mom!" I said, pushing her. "And I don't! What are you talking about? You don't know anything."

It was too late. Mom came into the kitchen, rubbing her eyes.

"Jill says you were out last night. Where were you?"

"Riding. Sorry, Mom."

"You can't leave Jill alone. It's not safe."

"I didn't mean to be gone so long."

"Don't do it again. And there's a phone message for you from Lisa. You must have missed it when you were feeding Meara. She said Roy's gone to the auction. She needs coffee beans and wants you to stop by the village's coffee bar on the way to the farm. Fanny, you're too young to be drinking coffee. You aren't, are you?"

I didn't answer. Just the thought of parking my bike in front of the coffee bar and walking into its heavy air made my chest tighten. Dad had always smelled of coffee. In the days that followed Dad's death, Mom had wandered the house, playing "Some Day Soon" over and over, carrying around a mug of coffee and a photo of him. I had stayed in my room, crying, not crying, feeling like I should be crying. Trying to memorize Dad. How his ears had stuck out under his Smithbilt. The feel of his stubble on my cheek. His raptor's profile sliding into a smile as he concentrated on making Mom laugh.

I fidgeted with my riding whip, nudging my boots with my toes. I could just see Mom where she stood in front of the kitchen window. Her hair, two shades darker brown than mine, was pulled into a severe ponytail and her shoulders hunched around her ribs like sparrows' wings.

"Fanny, I know you like this job. And we can sure use the money you're making. But six hours a day six days a week is too much for a teenager. Plus you're ignoring Jill and your chores here. When did you last read to her? Or give her a riding lesson? School starts in just a few weeks. Jill needs you, too."

I grabbed my lunch from the fridge and scuttled out the door. I could see Mom's angular frame, kettle in hand, through the window as I climbed on my bike. All the way to the coffee bar, I fretted. What would Mom think if Jill repeated her nonsense?

Lisa stood at her kitchen counter. "Thanks," she said, and dug in her purse for money as I handed her the beans. I had rushed in and out of the coffee bar to buy them without letting myself think about Dad. "It's hard to get out with the kids while Roy's got the truck. And he don't shop." Her voice was slow, almost a whisper.

It was the first time she'd addressed me directly. I covertly studied her face, wondering if she missed riding, but when she flicked her hair out of her eyes, I lost my nerve and didn't ask. In the hallway, the stroller, garish with dangling toys, blocked access to a door. Behind it, I could hear the twins, thumping and rough-housing. The air in the kitchen was as weighted as the inert baby on Lisa's hip. She moved like a lame horse, the baby's back slumped into the curve of her elbow, her free hand rattling beans into the grinder. "Want coffee?" The beans whirled, stopped. Her words dropped into the silence. "He ask you to go to Osoyoos?"

"Nero's waiting in the barn."

"He'll never let you ride in a race." Lisa's voice cracked, splinters following me out the door.

I groomed and saddled Nero, headed up the long hill toward Cultus Lake. What did she think about all day? How did she stand it, cooped up with those kids? I thought of Jill, how quick I'd been to leave her alone. Mom, burying herself in long hours at the cannery. Dad. He'd called us "his littlest bronc busters," had loved the hours he'd spent with us, Jill beside him as he'd shouted instructions to me aboard Meara.

On the grassy strip at the lake's edge, I stripped off the saddle, shed my jeans and dropped them in a heap, slid onto Nero's bare back. I told myself again that I'd never have kids as I kicked Nero's ribs, urging him into the lake. The water shocked away thought, then burned like ice. As Nero swam, my torso swayed, naked thighs tensed around his ribcage, my skin aching with more than cold. I believed I knew what Roy wanted when he watched me. No one had ever looked at me like that before.

When Nero plunged up the bank, we were both panting and breathless. I slid off and leaned against his shoulder, water dripping down my skin like melted glass, my legs jelly. I ran my hands down his tendons, one after another as Roy had taught me, lifted his hooves and picked them clean, then struggled back into my jeans for the soft ride back, my mind emptied.

Later that afternoon, Roy perched on the split rail fence, watching me untangle Nero's mane. He lit smoke after smoke, stubbing out each on the wooden post, and finally spoke. "You like speed, eh, girlie?"

I peered out at him from under Nero's neck, a currycomb in one hand. "So?"

His voice sharpened. "C'mon, you're finished there, quit fussin' and turn him loose. I'll run you home. Get in the truck." I hustled Nero out to the pasture and flicked the lead line off his halter. When I turned back, Roy was one-arming my bike over the tailgate of the truck, shouting towards the kitchen door. "Lisa! Running Fanny home, I'll eat when I get back." He yanked the door open. "Get in, get in. Come on, girlie. I swear, you're all alike. I ain't payin' you to lollygag."

The gearbox ground as he backed down the lane, shoved the truck into first at the road's edge and sharply hauled its nose east toward the village instead of west. The curtain across the bay window twitched. I jerked my face resolutely toward the windshield, my throat tensing.

"Gotta get me some smokes," Roy said. He stepped out of the cab in front of the corner store adjacent to the coffee bar. I watched as he walked away, then back, cigarette in mouth, light flickering as his face tilted down to the flame. When he lifted his head, he saw me looking. "You want one? No?" He cranked the ignition, sat back and puffed his cigarette as the truck roared, then he turned to face me. "So you ask your mom yet about Osoyoos? You do want to come, eh?"

"I want to, yes. But I haven't asked."

"Better get on with it, girlie. Or I'll find me another groom. No motel there, we sleep in the horse trailers. Bring a sleeping bag." He reached across the gearshift and put his right hand on my knee. He had extraordinarily long fingers. They stretched all the way around my kneecap, lying in the creases across my jeans.

"Maybe you can ride a race there after all, down in Osoyoos. You just think about that." He leaned back, plucked the cigarette from his mouth, shifted gears with it clutched between his fingers, turned the truck up the road. "You tell me the next couple a days."

I stumbled into the house, careful to avoid Mom, relieved for the first time that Dad wasn't around to cross-examine me. He'd have read my face like a schoolbook. When I headed for the shower, my jeans were still damp as I pulled them free of my knees. Later, I lay in bed and pondered the impossible. I couldn't ask my mother. I already knew what she'd say. I thought of Sheila, her laughing assurance. What would she do?

It rained the next day. My bedroom door tightly closed, I practiced the phrases I needed. At four, I sidled into the kitchen. Mom was peeling potatoes with her worn paring knife, the kitchen window smoggy with steam from the pot roast in the oven.

When I leaned against the cupboard, she lifted her head. "Hmm?"

"You want me to finish up so you can change for work?"

She steepled her eyebrows. "What do you want, Fan?"

"Roy and Lisa are going to the Osoyoos races. Roy says Lisa's going to be busy with the twins and the baby, visiting her parents, and he needs me to groom. Please, Mom." I was careful, with my tone, with my eyes, not looking at her.

"When?"

"In a couple weeks, just before before school starts. C'mon, Mom. You went to the rodeo down there when you were my age." The pulse beneath her left eye started to tic. Mentioning the rodeo was a mistake. I rushed to fill the moment. "I've been working all summer, Mom, I haven't gone anywhere. Dad always said that summer is for play, not just work. It would be good for me to have a change before school starts. And you, too. Just think how quiet the house will be with just Jill!"

At that, Mom laughed and the room lightened. "All right, I'll think about it. But it's a long way, honey, and that's a tough town."

"Mom, c'mon! Lisa's going to be there."

"We'll talk about it later, Fanny."

I snorted. Stomped across the porch and snatched my slicker. "We never talk about things when you say that!"

"Don't be long. Supper's at six."

The brambles along the driveway quaked as I slammed the door. When I got to Roy's barn, I flung my bike against the fence and grabbed a pitchfork. Work might block out what was bound to happen if Mom called Lisa. If she caught me in this lie, I'd be grounded forever and Mom would make me quit my job.

"Why do I get the indecisive mom?" I muttered as I stacked the wheelbarrow with bales and trundled it down the aisle of the barn. "Later, Fanny. Later, Fanny." Nero pricked his ears, watching me with interest over the stall door. I parked the wheelbarrow in the spare stall. Then I checked his hooves, flung a saddle and bridle on him and led him through the rain toward Roy's racetrack.

Lisa intercepted me at the gate. She wore a long black oilskin slicker and a pair of rubber boots protruded beneath it. Her hair shimmered with raindrops. It was the first time I'd seen her outside the house, without a child clinging to her. She looked like a horsewoman. Funny that I'd never imagined her astride a horse, even as I stood on her stool to mount her husband's horses.

"The track's like slop, Fanny. Roy'll have your guts for garters, and mine too, if you take Nero out there on a day like this. C'mon."

She took Nero's reins from my hands, led us both back into the barn, tied the gelding in the wide centre aisle. I picked his feet clean of mud and gravel, then stood at his head, twisting the reins in my hands. Beside me, Lisa unbuckled the girth and folded it on top of the saddle, her hands moving without hesitation across the leather. She looked up and caught my eye, shrugged and smiled. "Never thought I'd have a houseful of kids."

"I'm never having kids."

She grunted. Watching her deft fingers, I wanted to ask her what had happened. Why did she stay? But I couldn't get the words past an image of her husband's long hand on my knee. At the time, I didn't realize that she'd been pulled to the same flame that drew me. She slid the saddle from Nero's back, replaced the bridle with a halter, led him into the field and turned him loose. As he ambled off, we leaned side by side over the stall door, watching drops plunk into the wooden barrel just outside the barn. The horses, water beading on their slick coats, cropped grass beyond the gate, the air sweet with rain and freshly cut hay.

Lisa twirled the fraying lead line between her fingers. "He's had lots of exercise girls, y'know. They all leave sooner or later."

"I'm not just some exercise girl!"

"My point exactly." She wiped her hand across her face, her silver wedding ring gleaming. "Neither was I. Go home, Fanny."

I was shocked into silence. Lisa's words echoed, familiar somehow. When I could breathe again, Roy was standing in the doorway, his hat brim catching the rain.

"Go inside. The baby's awake," he said quietly. Lisa laid her hand on my forearm, then she edged past him like a skittish mare, the lead line dragging in the mud.

Roy looked at me steadily as water dripped past his cheekbones. "You stayin'? Them horses need their oats."

What would my dad make of Roy? I thought I knew, could hear his advice, echoing Lisa's, in my head. I set the saddle on the edge of the manger and slipped through the narrow doorway, careful to not let my jacket sleeve brush his. I swiped my bike seat dry with my cuff, looking up at the kitchen curtain at the same time. No movement.

Roy's boots crunched on the gravel. He snaked out an arm, gripped the handlebars in his long fingers. "Don't you forget to tell me about Osoyoos. By tomorrow. I still need a groom." I tugged my bike free and scrabbled through the wet stones towards the kitchen. Roy's voice growled behind me. "Don't you be botherin' her. She's got kids to tend. Git on home."

"I quit," I said.

In the flat light, his rain-spattered profile looked weathered, and I remembered the rain-streaked faces of my father's rodeo buddies as they flanked my mother at his graveside in Cloverdale. Every man there had been a fearless bull rider or bronc buster. That day, they'd all worn the haunted look of men who knew they had dodged death because of my father. No one had spoken except the minister. At the service's end, the men had patted my mother's shoulder, then strode to the waiting cars, their wives hanging back to deliver soft-voiced condolences and hugs.

I shuddered. It wasn't just Roy who looked old, but me. My face, reflected in the barn window, distorted by the running rain. I looked like my mother. Why had I never seen it before? My imagination painted in the squalling baby, the tussling kids. It was my future I was staring at.

In my chest, the birds quieted.

I waved towards the house, my arm swinging in a wide slow arc that encompassed everything. I meant it to convey gratitude to the woman standing behind the kitchen curtain, watching us. I would never stand in Lisa's kitchen again. Years later I would hear through the grapevine when she and Roy celebrated their twenty-fifth wedding anniversary, and I would hope that it wasn't bitter dregs for her. That rainy evening, pushing my bike down the long lane, I started to whistle to the horses behind the barbed wire, but stopped mid-breath, leaving them grazing in their field.

Undercurrents

I WAS CUTTING BACK THE SALAL along the driveway when the old VW made the turn off Black Creek Road. The young woman was the first to climb out, red braids tight-wrapped in a high crown above her forehead. She looked about her timidly before she reached back into the van, a little boy with strawberry blond curls squirming in her arms. An older couple — her folks? — emerged slowly from the VW, the woman's salt-and-ginger hair and dimmed-down face a pale variation of her daughter. The man gritted his teeth as he swung his hips clear on the driver's side of the faded Volks. Of course it was raining, that steady flat drizzle that draws in the horizon and absorbs any light. None of them wore rain gear. I leaned my weed-whacker against a cedar tree, went right over and put my hand on the toddler's chubby forearm. The young woman's grey eyes widened and she backed away. I took a step closer and rumpled the boy's hair.

"It's okay. Little kids like me. What is he, nearly two? Welcome to Miracle Beach Marina. Here, give him to me." Her arms and face tightened as I pulled the boy from her arms, surprised by his heft. He leaned away, then tilted his face up to look at me, curious. Dark blue eyes the colour of larkspur, eyelashes like a calf's. I smiled at him, then turned back to the others. "I'm Peter

Merrick. The owner." I jerked my head toward the office. "You folks look like you could use a little help right about now."

The younger woman backed up to stand behind her mother, her arms wrapped around her torso. She didn't look at me, but stood with her head down, gazing at my rubber boots. It was the braids, I thought, looking closely at her, that made her soft face seem older than she was. On closer study, I took her to be maybe seventeen.

The older woman smiled. Not everyone would, rain notwithstanding. She stuck out her right hand. It was hard with muscle and tight skin, fingernails bitten to the quick.

"We're the Harrises. My girl's Fiona, that's Joe," — the little guy obligingly wiggled in my arms at the sound of his name — "and I'm Sal. And Norm. It's been a long day, we got held up at the ferry terminal in Vancouver, hours and hours, and Joey ran us ragged . . ." The woman's voice fell. Her husband didn't look at me, just bent over his task as he tugged at a stroller buried behind the back seat. A brown and white beagle danced in the sand, avoiding human feet with yapping barks and sideways leaps. "Hush, Tag. Norm, say hi, won't you?"

Dog and man ignored her.

"Here, Red," I said, "why don't you take that little one into the marina, out of this rain for a bit, that's it just down the drive. You might not want to use the stroller, the sand's pretty soft. Been raining like crazy this month, it's driven half my guests away. Look, you can't miss it, the big cedar building. There's a hot chocolate and coffee machine by the main door, go get something hot and I'll just . . ." I put the damp boy back into her arms. "See ya soon, kiddo." Grabbed the stroller Norm had finally freed.

"You want an ocean view, right? Here, Norm, I'll show you a nice campsite. We'll have your tent pitched in no time."

None of them argued. Sal, one of those strong hands clutching her tall daughter's shoulder, never looked back. Fiona did, a quick glance as they made the turn at the cedars, but I couldn't see the expression on her face. The beagle jogged off behind them, stopping to look over its shoulder at Norm, who whistled, an odd two-tone. The dog came back and hopped into the back of the van while I pointed out a likely campsite to Norm. He didn't offer me a ride, so I hoisted the stroller and walked the path to the campsite while he drove around the lane and parked.

Tag curled under the arbutus tree next to the VW, nose on paws, while we hauled the tent bag out of the vehicle. Poles, clattering and clanking, tumbled onto the sparse grass that edged the sand. The tent was old and heavy. Canvas, its tears impeccably hand-mended, but still likely to leak.

I pried the story out of Norm. Not that I usually pry, but that gorgeous woman-child had caught my attention. Former Air Force, he said, raised on the east coast. No accent. Sal was from the prairies, she didn't understand how rain could fall all day, all night, and still be falling come morning. A year ago, he took early retirement. He stopped, hands stilled on the canvas. Looked at me. Red-rimmed eyes, pale as glacial runoff, edged with near-invisible eyelashes. Not a friendly stare.

"How early?" I asked.

"Not early enough."

A dishonourable discharge occurred to me as I took in his brush cut and the set of his jaw under a sheen of silver stubble as bristly as the haircut. He looked hard. He told me they had moved from base to base with Sal's beagle, the beds and the mahogany buffet he'd inherited from his grandmother.

"When Fiona graduated in June, I decided it was time. Put it all into storage in Cold Lake, up in northeastern Alberta. You know it?" I nodded. "I loaded the sleeping bags and tent into the van. We camped our way here. Fiona and Sal picked fruit for a few weeks in the Okanagan. And I lucked into a couple days' shop work in Merritt. A new life," Norm said, eying me as if he was daring me to challenge him, then he slipped through the mist and heavy cedars to find his family. I shrugged and followed.

A lot of drifters end up at seaside marinas, something about tough times draws folks to the water. Me, for instance. When the big crash almost shut down Calgary in the early eighties and Northern Eagle Oil and Gas bounced me from my highrise office, where did I end up? Here on the east coast of Vancouver Island, staring at the Georgia Strait as if I'd never seen water before. It's taken me the better part of three decades to fit in, but I never want to go back to corporate life. This marina and its small ebb and flow are enough. There's something about the light, so similar to the light in Alberta when the snow and sky were indistinguishable, only on the coast it's water and wind. The days blur past, and all I have to steer by are the folks coming into the marina looking for maps or coffee or a friendly voice.

Arlene didn't come west with me when I fell. Said she couldn't abide the thought of those closed-in mountain skies, she'd feel claustrophobic after living on the plains. Anyhow, she had better game in mind. She never said it quite that frankly, but she stayed in Calgary — last I heard, she married an oilman who hit it big in the tar sands up north. Guess I judged her wrong when I married her. So I just looked at the long-legged young women, their swinging hips and bright faces, and I got by; a few of them took a small shine to me and rubbed a little of their brightness onto my days. But none of them stuck either. It was just me sleeping in the loft above the marina.

I started with an oyster lease on Desolation Sound over on Cortes Island. It didn't look far on a map, but these coastal distances deceive. When the ferry rates went up again, I sub-leased it to a Portuguese kid whose family had been fishing salmon for decades. What he ships each week to those new yuppie restaurants in Vancouver and Calgary keeps us both in beer. It proved that old saying: when the tide's out, the table's spread. He supplies me with Miyagi oysters, and clams, and some mussels for the store, and I keep a few traps for Dungeness crab. The marina has a couple dozen campsites, set back from the gales, and the dock manages a handful of boats. That's plenty. I've never gone hungry, even through all those lean years after I left Calgary. The salmon fishery is dying, but folks still come to the sea.

By the time I reached the marina, all four stragglers looked revived. The little guy, Joe, was running around the store, reaching for fishing reels and nets as if he was born to the oceanside. The others were leaning on the counter, empty mugs beside their hands, examining maps and copies of the local rag. When I came in, they all turned to me, questions in their eyes.

"Ten bucks a night to pitch your tent, free access to the showers and firepits. There's wood stacked under the lean-to out beside the shower building. Washers and dryers, a loonie a load. Another three bucks a night if you want to plug in. Or do you have a generator?"

Norm answered, reserved in front of his women. "Nah, but we've got our Coleman lantern and stove."

I'd seen them in the VW as we unraveled gear looking for tent pegs, and they'd looked as ancient — but as carefully tended — as the tent itself.

"No worries. How about a couple bucks off on account of the lousy weather?" I asked, and out of the corner of my eye, I saw Sal's face soften with relief. And I wondered again. Whose kid was the little boy? Had to be Red's. Sal seemed too old, but if he was Red's, why was she raising him on her own?

It was like her mother read my mind and didn't like the lettering.

"Fiona, we better get Joey out of here before he breaks something." Sal had regained her poise, and moved as gracefully as the teenager to swoop up the child, gently tugging a wicker creel from his fat fingers. "Thanks, mister — ?"

"Merrick. But just call me Peter. I'm up here if you need anything. At all." I waved my arm at the shelves stocked with canned goods and produce. "I'm a little closer than the grocery stores in Merville or Comox, and frankly, ladies, my produce is better. Francisco brings down fresh shellfish and tuna from up-island three times a week, and I have some local lamb in the deep freeze if you get tired of seafood. If you want, I can show you where to harvest oysters, just around the point a bit . . . ever eat an oyster, kiddo?" Joe was wide-eyed and silent as I smiled at him on his perch on Sal's hip.

Norm pulled bank notes from his worn wallet.

"A month?"

I nodded. "Sure thing. The off-season and long-stay rates are better. September is shoulder season, that's half of your month.

Here." I pushed some bills back at him. He pocketed them without looking up. "Sorry about the rain. It's settled in early this year." Only Joe looked back as they left the building, his round face cracking wide in a pumpkin's grin when he caught my eye.

After dinner, rain sheeting off the windows, I sat with a Scotch by the fire and spun tales for myself, inventing possible scenarios, ignoring the implications. They all involved a long-legged redhead. A chubby child played at the periphery like a question mark.

I was up early the next morning. I had a hot pot of coffee and empty mugs in my hands when I made my customary rounds down the narrow footpath and across the boardwalk to the campground. We had pitched the tent in a quiet little dell, fronted by a stand of Douglas firs, well past the half dozen other tents and trailers clustered by the shower building that stood a stone's throw from the lodge. I waved to an early morning jogger heading past the firs to the straits, where a long path led past the high tide driftwood and the blanket of kelp that washed up against the logs. The rain hadn't stopped, gleaming droplets on the salal leaves like water on a cold gin bottle. At the trail to the Harris' site, spiky stalks of berries glowed, miniature mauve lanterns. I stooped, stripped some into an empty mug.

Fiona was squatting before the firepit and a black cast iron griddle, hissing and spitting bacon, pancakes bubbling.

"Mornin'." I spoke first.

"Morning."

Her hair hung loose now, like spun red gold. All I could think of were old fairy tales. Rumpelstiltskin. A beauty and a dwarf. Blackbeard. Another Beauty in the Beast's kingdom. I wanted to ask her how she'd slept. Did the roar of the surf keep her awake, did the leaks from the tent ceiling miss her back, if the child had fussed. Instead, I held out both hands — coffee and ripe berries. Gifts.

She laid the flipper down on the stones beside the griddle but kept hold of its handle. "No thanks."

"Tried them already, did you? Sour, aren't they? You gotta cook them, they make wicked jelly. At the farmers' market, local women can't keep up when the Oregon grapes are in season. How about some coffee instead?" I gestured with the pot. "Fresh made, good beans, break your Starbucks city girl heart."

She laughed, looked at me briefly, then quickly down. She stood up. We were the same height exactly. When she took a cup from my hand, I prayed silently. God, don't let her turn from my ugly face. God, don't let her.

"I have some spare time, thought you and the little guy might want a look at the beach. I can show you the safe spots to splash and where the riptide can pull you back out to the straits. Water safety for new arrivals."

"Joey's still sleeping." She tipped her head back toward the tent. "My folks are pretty done in too."

"Your dad looks the type to never admit he's getting on. The little guy must be a constant reminder, Red."

"Don't call me that!"

"Sorry. Fiona, then. It's just that you remind me of Rita Hayworth. The movie star?"

She shook her head, flushing, her lips tightening, then looked down at the bacon that was spitting fat across her hand. "What's a riptide?"

"An undertow." Her face stayed bent, so I kept on, trying to smooth over the flood I felt. "An undercurrent that runs seaward from the shore. It can drag you out to deep water, flows nearly three meters per second. That's fast." I was starting to sound like a professor, but I kept talking. Better boredom than the tension that had rushed through her at the mention of her father. "It's strongest near the surface, not under the water. All you have to do is swim parallel to it and angle back to shore. But it's pretty risky for little kids."

By the time her mother emerged from the tent, yawning, Fiona's face was smooth again, the bacon was moved to cool on the edge of the firepit, and I had elicited a promise of a walk that afternoon to investigate water flow and tidal pools. I set the full pot down on the grill and left them the empty cups, careful to turn away before a set of gunmetal blue maternal eyes could bore into me.

As I walked away, Fiona called. "Mister Merrick?"

"Peter. Call me Peter."

"Do you have a kid's rain jacket I could borrow for Joey? Please?"

She's too young, I told myself harshly. But that didn't keep me from promising to bring a child's jacket and pants with me when I came back.

A faded driftwood gate the same colour as Fiona's eyes marked the way to the beach. I hung across its arm and watched them play. At first, Tag kept close to Fiona, who crouched to watch the interminable crawl of whelks through a tiny current carved in the hard-packed sand. Out ahead, Joe squatted, stick in hand, digging through the damp seaweed, ignoring washed-up starfish and sand dollars and scuttling tiny crabs, intent on extricating a piece of bull kelp. I jogged over and knelt beside him.

"Hi, Joey. Remember me?"

He nodded, intent on his task.

"Need some help?"

"Me do." His voice was soft. He tugged the kelp loose and held it out to me.

"Belk."

"Kelp, Joey. You can crack it. Like a whip." I waved my arms and a passing sheltie, its owner a distant figure in rain gear and gumboots, mistook my motion for an invitation. She bounced and bowed on her forelegs at Joe. Joe, looking worried, scrambled up the adjacent log and into my arms. He touched my unshaven cheek with round fingers before climbing down as the dog ran off.

He struggled with the long bull kelp. "Kep."

"You got it, Joe. Kelp."

Joe dragged the heavy length of seaweed down the beach towards Fiona, the dog forgotten. Clambering over a log, he slipped and landed knees-first on some wrack, gasped but didn't cry, distracted as the seaweed deflated with a pop. He peered intently under his knees, then systematically stomped it into pulp. Tag ran between Joe and Fiona, maddened by the rain, ears flopping as she barked and growled. At the water's edge, she chased the receding line of foam as the waves washed over the sand and stones. But she stayed well back of the surf.

"Smart dog, eh, Joey?" The little boy grinned at me from under his hood, his cheeks beading with water. Despite the pouring rain, Fiona was smiling too.

"I've never seen the sea before. Mom and Gran grew up on a farm in Saskatchewan," Fiona told me as Joe took off after Tag. "Stony-ass broke, Mom says. She doesn't talk so much anymore, but she and Gran used to tell stories. My favourite was about riding the old horse to school." Her grey eyes met mine. Her first direct look at me. Smiled, her face as unguarded as her son's. "But Gran liked to tell me about killing chickens. You know they run around without any heads after she chopped 'em to death on the block? Do you believe that? I can't get it out of my mind." She bent and scooped up the squealing boy. "Crazy, eh, Joey? And then Gran's dogs went crazy. No water to drink. They'd love it here, it's so wet! And doesn't it smell good?" She buried her nose in Joe's belly and blew raspberries. He giggled.

I winced. She was too young all right, and too young to tell such grim stories, with the twang of want that ran through them. Sal had been quick to ask me that morning just what was free for harvesting and what needed a license. Oysters and clams were free.

A day later, I looked out the window of my office and saw the girl and the little boy walking toward the beach, buckets in hand. The VW was nowhere to be seen. Fiona led the way. Tag bounced and dodged when Joe threw his galvanized bucket onto the stones with a clanging racket. It was low tide. I strained to watch them until they vanished out of sight around the promontory. I knew what they'd be doing, same as I had done when I arrived: swarming across the slick rocks, heading for the open stretch of hard-packed sand where the sea retreated. Just beyond were more rocks, where oysters lay in plain sight for the taking, their wet layers ridges of calcified time. Emptied shells, reminiscent of bones and glowing as if they had a half-life, were heaped behind the marina by the firepit.

I grabbed my slicker and locked up. Doubled back and grabbed a new one off the shelf for Fiona. Weather was coming. I caught up with them a couple hundred meters down the beach and took the bucket from Joe's small hands.

"C'mon, Joey, run! Faster!" Fiona shrieked as they leaped from log to log. When I caught up with them, Joe wordlessly held up his arms. I slung him on one hip and used the other hand to drape the rain jacket around Fiona's shoulders. Her clothes smelled like salt and smoke. She shivered when my fingers brushed her arm.

"Don't get cold," I said, and kicked myself for unsettling her.

That night, I lay in my quiet bed and brought the flesh of my upper arm to my nose, imagining and inhaling the smeared scents overlaying Fiona's skin. Through the open window, I heard gravel churn as the VW's headlights poured into the parking lot. I thought I heard a raised voice, the fire crackling.

Fiona stopped me on the boardwalk the next morning, heading back to the campsite from the marina. Norm, a few yards ahead, halted and leaned against a cedar, watching us. His cigarette glowed.

"Peter! You should have warned me about the slugs!" Fiona shuddered. "Good thing I put my rubber boots on first thing." Slugs like it beneath the Oregon grapes and ferns beside the path, their slow silver tracks a hint of secret deeds. The trip to the showers and toilets should not be undertaken half-asleep or barefoot. "Our blankets never quite dry out," she grumbled. "Does it rain here all the time? I don't know if the smell of mould will ever come out of them." What worried me was how her father's eyes followed her, leaving their own snail's trail.

On the final day of August, the VW pulled up in front of the marina store. Norm sat impassively in the driver's seat, smoking, flipping through the want ads while Fiona struggled to lift Joe out of the car seat. As soon as the van's doors closed, Norm pulled away. I speculated about where he was heading as Sal approached the counter.

"Just Norm's ciggies, Peter. And choose some nice apples for Joey, Fiona," she said as Joe wandered through the aisles. Fiona smiled at me. Joe ran up holding a plastic fishing rod. I winked at Fiona and shuffled through cigarette cartons for a packet of Player's.

"Hey, Joey, you like that rod?" I directed my question halfway between the women. Neither answered, then Fiona whisked the toy from Joe's hands. Her face flushed as she put it back on the shelf. "How's the job search going?" I asked Sal. "This rain sure is good beachcombing weather. Nice for those two," I said as I handed over the smokes.

"Nice has nothing whatsoever to do with it, Peter," Sal snapped. "Fiona comes back starving, she eats like a horse, and Norm hasn't found a decent job yet. We're still just on his severance. I don't know what I'll feed her and Joey. Pancakes only take a growing child so far."

"Here, Sal. Put this on their pancakes tomorrow morning." I put a tin of maple syrup on the counter along with the change.

Sal hung her head. "Sorry, Peter, I don't know what got into me."

"Ah, don't worry about it, Sal. We all get a little crazy in the rain the first time. And in a tent? Sheesh. Tell Norm there's a new B&B opening near Cumberland, one of those agri-tourism places, might need a farmhand. I can give him the number if . . . "

I watched Fiona walk to the far end of the store to squint at a full-size fishing rod and didn't hear the answer.

A few hours later I was drinking my afternoon coffee on the bench in front of the marina, watching the rain trickle off the canopy. Through a dripping frame of Spanish moss, I saw Fiona by the woodpile, her arms full. Norm emerged from the shower building behind her. Instead of taking the wood from her, he ran his fingers down the sleeve of her slicker. She jerked her arm as if she'd been scalded, dropped the wood and ran, not stopping as she passed me.

"She needs a patch on that jacket you gave her. Leaks like a sieve," Norm said, deadpan, hands empty as he walked into the parking lot. I clenched my fist around my mug. As soon as the van's rear lights disappeared down the driveway, I hauled the abandoned wood to the campsite and stacked it tidily beside the fire. Sal, astride a bench peeling apple slices and feeding them to Joe, watched without saying a word, her mouth tight. The tent's canvas wall quavered.

That evening, at the pub in Comox, ale in my hand, I saw Norm walk in alone. A terse nod at me, and he strode to the bar without a word.

"The usual, Norm?"

I was gone before he looked around.

The unseasonable rain was relentless. My morning rounds through the campsite revealed that the damp had started to seep through the tent's roof and was puddling in the trenches Sal dug to channel away the water. Tag smelled increasingly doggy, and I worried that the driftwood logs were slick as ice under Fiona's sneakers. Norm and the VW were never in evidence when I crossed the boardwalk, and I began to question more and more just how he spent his days while his family made do in a small tent.

Out on the waterfront, the clams hid their spouting necks from the patrolling herons and gulls. Fiona and Joe picked dozens of oysters, then hunkered down, jackets steaming by the fire, Fiona's quick hands shucking the way I'd shown her, Joe stacking the empty shells in unstable piles. Sal found ways to serve them, drizzled with lemon, dashed with Tabasco. Scalloped and fried and dolloped with tartar sauce. For stew, I sold Sal a big cast iron pot for next to nothing, showed her how to bury its blackened base in the embers, and made the first batch. I threw in handfuls of onion and chunks of butter that hissed as the rain spat down. Bay leaves, thyme, milk, cubed potatoes, and then the oysters Fiona had patiently opened. Once cooked, they emerged milky and fat, scooped into deep bowls. Fiona's long fingers grazed mine as I handed her the stew.

"Quick, Fee!" I said, stumbling over my words to disguise the jolt of electricity I felt. "Eat it before the crackers get soggy."

Sal made stew by the gallon, briny-sweet and cloying, scented by the sea breeze as it blew in off the beach. Every evening, Norm steamed oysters open on the firepit's grill, the midden of discarded shells attracting the gulls. I was a frequent guest at their table, maybe as payback for the maple syrup and morning coffee. Sal refused my cautious offers of anything else, but I stashed chocolate bars in my jacket pocket for the little guy, who spooned down the broth and potatoes and even the oysters before turning to me expectantly. Norm's squinting eyes followed his wife, his daughter, but never tracked the movements of little Joe.

Fiona gagged one night when Sal served yet another pot of stew. As her daughter retched at the edge of the fire, Sal pivoted away.

"No more, Mom," Fiona said. "No stew. Not one more oyster, raw or steamed or broiled or grilled." Her father raised his head and studied his daughter.

I got up from the picnic table and patted Fiona's back. "Don't worry about it, Fee." I said, too softly for Sal to hear. "I'm sick of 'em too. You can use my rod anytime you want. I'll teach you. No more oysters." I rubbed small circles between her shoulder blades. The muscles eased a little but she didn't answer.

The bats came out. Joe ran around the campground, shrieking with glee, arms outstretched, as the bats hummed and whistled above him. Norm flicked his glowing cigarette butt towards them, then turned his back. The rest of us stood mesmerized, watching the glow fade into ash on the sand.

I was hosing salt crystals and sand off the marina walls when I saw two figures head out, buckets and shovels in hand. Fiona's hair shone in the watery sunlight.

"Dad says I should go out to the clam beds if I'm too good to eat oysters."

I shook my head with disgust.

"Don't worry about it, I'll teach you how to dig them, Fiona. I don't know why I didn't think of it earlier. It's easy as picking oysters."

I showed her how to wait for the squirts of water that betray the presence of the hidden clams. As soon as her spade entered the stony sand, another spout would erupt a few feet away. Joe, distracted, ran from pillar to post, Tag at his heels, both yipping like banshees. But Fiona quickly learned the dance: a few steps to the new spray, bend, dig quickly, and toss the clam into the bucket.

"Sluice off the sand and cover them with seaweed before you carry 'em back," I suggested. The pail was already half full when I left them there and headed back.

Twenty minutes later, I looked up to see Norm's silhouette, smoke drifting behind him as he passed along the beachhead. It wasn't long before Fiona re-appeared, bent nearly double, tugging and jerking the full bucket along the boardwalk and up the sandy path toward the firepit. She grinned and waved me off when I stuck my head out the door with an offer of help.

I was immersed in accounts receivable when I heard her crying, and her feet on the boardwalk. I dropped my pen and ran out.

"Fiona! What? What is it?"

She could barely speak, her breath gasping.

"I asked him . . . asked him . . . he nodded . . . so I . . . and Mom said . . . Mom said . . ."

"What, Fiona? Hush, hush. Calm yourself, here, sit down. Catch your breath. Nothing to be done until you can talk." I patted her onto the log bench and waited. "So. Now tell me. What did your mother say to you?"

"She said, 'Where's Joe? Where's your dad?' But, Peter, it was how she said it."

I had a sharp memory of the despair I'd seen in Sal's face as she fed apple slices to Joe against that backdrop of trembling canvas. I grabbed Fiona's hand and we ran, our feet slipping on the wet boardwalk.

I heard Tag barking hysterically as we approached the beach.

We rounded the curve past the highwater logs. A small stick lay beside a squiggle of lines drawn through a shallow runnel of water. Clouds banked above the distant coastline.

Even without my glasses I could see the child's golden hair glinting in the flat light. I slowed, tugged Fiona to a stop.

"He's okay, he's all right," I bent forward, gasping. Fiona pulled her hand free and ran, red hair flying.

"Joey!"

My feet and lungs were lead, but I ran after her all the same, cursing my age, cursing the heavy sand, cursing her father. Norm stood immobile, staring across the strait, cigarette in his mouth. Tag was racing back and forth along the lacy edge of the waves, a scant five feet from Norm, to where Joe sat, legs crossed like a tiny Buddha, the swirling water sucking sand and stones from beneath him.

The Bridge

At four am, Breathless rolls over and stares at the blue numbers on the clock. She can feel sweat beading on her upper lip. At five, she pulls on a skirt, tank top, sandals. Cigarettes and lighter, cash and key, cotton sweater over her arm. The hall floor creaks as she tiptoes to the lobby.

"Which way to the Brooklyn Bridge?"

The night clerk's smile is as wan as the walls. "A good half hour south on foot, ma'am. You aren't walkin' alone, surely?"

Breathless almost smiles. "I've seen things. It's like wearing armour, you know? A map, please."

The map materializes. "It's got the subways on the other side. See? And maybe I can lock your necklace in the hotel safe?"

"Gotcha. I'll keep it out of sight." She wraps her sweater sleeves around her throat, covering the necklace, steps into the morning.

A postcard pinned to the wall above the coffee urn in her favourite diner at home in Calgary had brought her to New York City. She'd stared at that postcard over breakfast for years. Men in hard hats and undershirts, building the mile-long Brooklyn Bridge over the East River in 1883, leaning casually on the cables. All those strands spoke volumes, braided steel wires that held the bridge together, tied it to the earth, stronger than they appeared, complicated beyond unstringing or understanding. The men who had woven the bridge into being were long dead, but Breathless had wanted to see their world — boots swinging over the bridge deck as they unpacked metal lunch buckets, at ease, unconcerned by the river, its currents, the city's unseen risks. As if life was no more demanding or perilous than a simple walk across a bridge. As if all anyone needed was a single silver strand to hold them safe and guide them home.

Home's a myth. Just the act of living takes all of her breath and attention. In her teens, Breathless would reluctantly pull herself from the shelter of a novel, arrive late for class, for supper, for visits with friends, her breath huffing, her face pink with the effort of being present. Her mother, a hardcore boozer, single all her life, dead forty years, had nicknamed her only daughter Breathless, abandoning the name she'd given her at birth. Breathless has always been grateful for that anonymity.

The streetlights are still flickering. Breathless scans the map, gets her bearings and heads to Stuyvesant Square, hoping for parkland, a fountain. But the park is tiny, stitched with paving stones and benches, a pair of magnolia trees. In front, a plain red building, the plaque announcing the Quaker meeting hall. Beside it, a Gothic heap of stone, complete with lions at the gates — the Episcopalians. Newspaper sheets crumpled on a bench ruffle in the breeze, a couple huddled beneath the folds, pillowed by corrugated cardboard. She tugs her sweater free, drops it on the forms huddled on the bench, doesn't look back when she hears a muttered "Thanks."

The breeze whispers across her bare neck, across the necklace, a lacework of silver filigree around a square-cut amethyst that reminds her of early-spring flowers. It's all Breathless has from her lover, Simon, a university prof, with a graceful neck and throat like a Canada goose, grey-haired, a fine down of silver hair on his chest. He'd whistled Sonny Rollins riffs in bed, scattered books and coffee rings around the hotel rooms they frequented, and left her abruptly, before the crocuses bloomed.

For her fiftieth birthday, they'd spent the afternoon at a riverside restaurant. He'd given her the necklace, clipping it around her throat where the stone pressed, cool against her skin, and then he'd retreated. "So long, sport," he'd said, as if it was the wind-up game of baseball season. "You're great, just great. It's been . . . well, I won't be seeing you again. Sorry."

Breathless had the impulse to throw the necklace at him as he left, but it had seemed pointless. Instead, she'd ordered coffee and madeleines, then walked home along Memorial Drive, the chain heavy on her neck. As she had crossed the footbridge over the river, she'd thought again about tossing the necklace away, but it already felt familiar, like the ache, a beacon to loss, buried beneath the stone.

Next day in the diner, her breakfast had sat untouched and her coffee cooled as she'd stared at the bridge in the postcard. At work, she'd gone online and spent her tips on a plane ticket.

As Breathless ambles down Fourteenth Street, at the corner of Second Avenue a woman surfaces from a brimming dumpster emblazoned with "Property of NYC," clutching a stained chenille bathrobe, her hinge of a voice scraping against the dumpster's metal walls. "What you starin' at?"

Breathless shrugs, keeps walking. How could she help? At Third, a street sweeper grinds past, its brushes scrubbing the pavement. In its wake of silence, a cop car rolls alongside her, window down. A hard brush-cut emerges. "You workin'? Move along."

She folds her arms. Raises her eyebrows. "Excuse me?"

"Oh, sorry, ma'am. This isn't the best neighbourhood. Maybe you should . . . " The head retreats.

Cops. Alike in any city. Plenty of them hang around at The Eddy, the east-side Calgary hotel where Breathless tends bar and keeps a small apartment on the second floor, home since Gran died. Her room is clean but sparse — a red Japanese paper lantern, narrow bed covered with Gran's patchwork quilt, a few clothes hanging in the closet. In the bathroom, a tawny orchid flowers for months at a time, something delicate but foreign about its stamens and intricate petals, evoking tropical nights, the waning moon. Exile.

Approaching Union Square, a pretzel vendor sets up for business in the lea of the market. Breathless imagines a horse harnessed to the cart, its nobbled head nodding, the huckster's thin shout cracking the early light. "Mustard. Salt. Hot pretzels. Get yer hots here."

The pretzel, still warm, is chewy, salty and dense inside, akin to Gran's bread. Her memory of Gran is fading, like the rug in her bedroom. Gran raised her after Breathless' mother had died. She hadn't been one for wasting anything — not fabric, not words, and her spare shows of affection had extended to plaiting rugs from scraps for Breathless' floor. Eating takeout noodles alone in her room after work, the knotty texture of the rug under her bare feet was a reassurance. She still felt. Something still stirred, might yet flare.

Horns blare through the morning air. Pickups and vans are backed up to the sidewalks lining Union Square, apron-wrapped men unloading flats of bread, links of sausages, tubs of cut flowers, onto tables and stalls.

"What's all this?" she asks one of the men when he looks up.

"It's Saturday, right? Farmers' market."

"How much for the flowers?"

"We ain't open for an hour yet. Here. Just take 'em." He grabs a bunch of tulips, jams them toward her.

"That's so kind! Which way to the subway station?"

"Yeah, no worries." He waves at a sign across the square. The tulips' orange tips bulge beyond their paper jacket. She tucks them under her arm and crosses the park for the subway, the bridge her final destination.

At the top of the stairs into the subway, a girl shoves past. She's maybe fifteen but her face is leathery with scars. A stride past, she swivels.

"You spare a few bucks? I haven't eaten in days."

Breathless assesses her short skirt and thin camisole, burn holes in the tights pulled across narrow thighs, holds out the tulips, and a ten. "Go get a juice and a bagel, girlfriend."

The girl ignores the flowers, grabs the bill. "I ain't your girlfriend, bitch." Her ankles wobble above her high heels as she retreats.

Girls like her hang out down the hall in The Eddy. Breathless is cautious there, coming and going, dodging needles and empty syringes, stepping around the girls clustered in the stairwell. When she'd arrived in Calgary at nineteen, she'd found a similar room in a similar hotel, and had offered several similar girls a cot and bite to eat, but her jewellry and clothes had disappeared with them. She's learned to nod and say hi, looks past their bruises, and as casually as she can, she gives them juice boxes, peanuts from the bar. Their stagnant faces remind her of her mother, her breath and body heavy with gin, snoring on the couch while Breathless scrambled together her school lunch.

The subway station's stairwell needs a good paint job and the floors need a mop. Breathless buys a token and feeds the turnstile, wanders through the cavernous halls and corridors until she finds a map threaded with colours. The platform for number six downtown is nearly empty. Breathless leans on a cement pillar, studying the wall tiles, their chipped enamel fading. Thirty years of looking away from girls who could've been her, tending bar and dating a string of men, listening to minor plans and lies. Whenever Breathless would look in the mirror back home, she'd wonder why she hadn't succumbed to dope or booze. What does she have to show for surviving? Back home, The Eddy's regulars lean on the counter, certain of her ear. "Breathless, listen. This guy at work, he tells me one day . . ."

Tom, the acerbic manager, would inevitably flip his ponytail, snort and ask, "You got a candy-ass heart? See yourself as some shrink, gonna save the world?" He doesn't have the patience to wait for the stories that leak onto the bar, but he sees the tip jar fill each evening during her shift.

"I'm here anyways, Tom," Breathless always shrugs. "I might as well listen." There isn't much she hasn't heard. Sometimes she feels numb, although the stories keep her from fretting about aging alone, and although her cheeks are still firm and high, her breasts too, some mornings, lying on her bed, her bones ache, and she's not looking thirty anymore, her hair slipping from mahogany to mouse.

"Maybe your next big thing is to set up some charity house for them girls, hmm?" Tom heckled the day before she flew to New York. "Become a Mother Teresa."

Breathless laughs at the thought.

When the train chuffs to a halt, Breathless steps through the doors and takes a window seat. She averts her eyes when a clutch of young men in tight black jeans and jackets scramble through the door, the sweet stink of stale alcohol wafting from their clothing. One lags behind, appraising Breathless. He jerks his chin at her.

"How 'bout it?"

"In your dreams." She settles by a window, her hand rubbing the smooth stone at her throat. The door hisses shut and the young man sways up the aisle into the seat behind her. He's older than he seemed, scarred and bruised, dull eyes. For a minute, she watches his reflection in the window, tries to breathe smoothly, looking for an escape route. But she still jumps when his hand grabs her hair at the nape of her neck, turns her face inexorably towards his.

"C'mon. You want it." He wraps his forearm around her throat.

The ripcord panic line is out of reach above her head. His friends cluster at the far end of the car, watching as he forces her to her feet. She retreats, step by step, until her back is against the central door, the man crowding her, his breath bitter, leaning in, his thighs hard. Breathless tries to jam her knee upward into his crotch, an elbow pinned to her ribs.

His hand tightens around her throat. Breathless thinks of Gran, her muscular forearms, as the car slows to a stop. The door behind her opens and frees her arm. She whips the tulips up, a hard backhanded arc that lands her knuckles on the point of his nose and the flowers in his eyes.

"Bitch!" He jerks back, then sneezes.

Breathless almost forgets to move, then pulls free, stumbles through the doorway, smashed flowers tumbling through the gap to the tracks. She looks back, catches sight of him, regains her balance and runs across the empty platform, up the stairs, no second chances, no echoing footsteps.

Above ground, the sun shimmers behind the mist, damp air a welcome touch on her skin. Breathless eases her pace, arms wrapped around her heaving ribcage, shuddering as she approaches the curved crosswalk to the bridge. Even on an early weekend morning, the car deck below is busy. Along the elevated walkway, the wooden slats under her feet are dull, but the cables above her head twang like bluegrass chords.

At the sound of footsteps chasing up behind her, Breathless convulsively hunches, ducking. Two women in jogging gear, wired, feet moving in unison. They nod, a kind of salute. When they pass Breathless, she studies their square-held backs, her shoulders loosening in their hinges.

From the east, out of the shadows hanging over Brooklyn, a man in a tattered beige trench coat leads a little dog. The man moves with a lurching reel, as if he's been too many years in dry dock. The dog, an apricot poodle, shambles to a halt at her shin, and cocks its hind leg.

"Hey! Get on!" The man yanks the leash. The dog reluctantly lowers its leg and disappears up the sidewalk, the man staggering along in its wake.

Breathless paces to where wires and cables coalesce. In the postcard, this spot is the heart of the bridge, where workmen rubbed elbows, their rough community palpable. In the exact centre, a sax player stands alone. His music hangs, smoky as the light. Breathless stops, leans on the rail, waits for her heart to settle, watching his long fingers on the stops, listening as he riffs. He cocks an eyebrow and nods at her without lifting his mouth from the reed.

"'Giant Steps'?" Her voice is a whisper.

The player nods again, lips pursing around the reed. He's grey-haired, weathered, with the angular body of a basketball player, clad in t-shirt and chinos, his torso bending with the music he blows. His fingers slide from metal to metal as if the instrument is skin and soul.

When the music stops, she drops a folded bill into the open instrument case lying at his feet.

"No need," he says. "I play for my own pleasure."

Pleasure seems a long way away. Breathless turns to the view on the Manhattan side, to the Chrysler Building's majestic indifference. Tears slide down her cheeks. So many losses. Youth, lovers, opportunity, Gran, her ruined mother, hope, all the unwinding threads of her life. The tulips on the subway tracks. Then she looks up at the bridge's silver wires, spinning their own web above the city, its tugboats, stevedores and smugglers, their stowed secret cargo, broken, beautiful and tragic. Incomprehensible irony.

The music follows Breathless as she walks back into Manhattan. To the first open coffee vendor, next to its furled umbrella, sipping, pondering the scars on the jazz blower's naked forearms, what he has seen, how he continues to play.

She lifts her half-full mug in acknowledgment, tells the barista, "Another, a double to go, extra hot," then strides back up the bridge, balancing both cups in a cardboard tray. He's still there, Rollins rolling from his horn as if the big man himself still straddled the bridge. Breathless sets the extra cup beside the musician's feet, nods to him, walks to the rail. Halfway through "St. Thomas" the sax player bends, drinks, missing barely a beat as he straightens. Notes slide from the horn, channeling Coltrane, Rollins, Parker. Breathless follows the melody into the beautiful depths, thinking about the centuries of differences between men and women, their desolations and separate longings.

She reaches behind her neck to unclip the silver chain holding her amethyst. Coffee cup in one hand, her elbow balanced on the bridge's cable, her necklace lies across her palm, fingertips fretting where stone and silver meet. All Breathless is conscious of, all she can absorb, is that its strands will tarnish and the amethyst will loosen in its setting. Letting go might be easier.

Finally he stops playing. Removes the strap and the reed, lays the saxophone in its bed. He tenderly wipes the metal clean, then he strides toward her, his head gently bobbing, eyes blinking behind round glasses. An arm's length away, he stops.

Breathless freezes.

His hands open at waist height, palms up. Her breath whistles as he plucks the necklace from her hand, opens it. Without touching her, his arms encircle her. Deft fingers attach the clasp at the nape of her neck. "Just don't quit," he murmurs, rough as unrehearsed music. "You hear?" Calloused fingertips brush across the amethyst in the hollow at the base of her throat. He swings back to his sax in its case. Picks it up and begins to play.

Breathless, feeling oddly blessed, lights a smoke, leans on the spun wire railing, her fingers on the silver chain. Downriver, she can make out the Statue of Liberty. Light undulates along the river's milky skin. She can sense the sky, the city's vast inhale as real as her own skin's rise and fall above her ribs. Chin on her forearms, she feels New York surrounding her. Above her shoulder, the long-gone workmen are still a presence, tangible in the wires they strung. She can hear them now, her ear softened by the big man's playing. As her cigarette burns down to the filter, she smiles ruefully, her boss' offhand comment echoing. Maybe she is a do-gooder after all. Considers the cost of a few rooms next to hers in The Eddy, a shelter, a safe landing for those homeless girls. The stub of her cigarette flicks free and she watches the firefly tumble and spark of its descent, like sparks from a welder, until it disappears into the river.

When Breathless walks back to the jazz player, he half-smiles, his face tipped toward her above his sax, inviting.

"Lucinda," she says, nodding in time to the music inside her, the bridge's wires singing far above. "My name. It's Lucinda," and it seems to her that he weaves those three syllables into his song while the river runs on to where water and sky blur into horizon.

Acknowledgments

"Monroe's Mandolin" was published in *The Antigonish Review*, summer 2011, Vol. 166

"The Quinzhee" was a shortlisted finalist for *The Malahat Review*'s 2009 Far Horizons Short Fiction Award, and in *FreeFall*'s 2011 open short fiction contest. It was published as "The Quinzie" in *FreeFall*, spring 2012, Vol. XXII, No. 2.

"Undercurrents" was published in *The Malahat Review*, summer 2011, Vol. 175

"The Good Husband" was a shortlisted finalist in *FreeFall*'s 2012 open short fiction contest.

"Still Life with Birds" was a shortlisted finalist in *The New Quarterly*'s 2012 Peter Hinchcliffe Short Story Contest.

An early version of "Exercise Girls" was a runner-up with Honourable Mention for the 2009 Brenda Strathern Late Bloomers Creative Fiction Award.

The Saskatchewan Arts Board, Access Copyright, and Sage Hill Writing provided much-appreciated financial assistance.

To my brilliant, fey, fierce, and generous editor, Seán Virgo, "Go raibh maith agat."

Many of these stories were begun or concluded at the Saskatchewan Writers' Guild colonies at Emma Lake and St. Peter's Abbey. Two were written at Wallace Stegner House in Eastend. Thanks to the province's writers and artists for adopting me.

Thank you to Guy Vanderhaeghe, Johanna Skibsrud, and especially Sandra Birdsell.

Dave Carpenter and Honor Kever, for quinzhees, constructive criticism, many kindnesses and friendship. Philip Adams and Yvette Nolan.

My colleagues in Visible Ink, especially Andréa Ledding and Lisa Bird-Wilson.

Jeanette Lynes, professor and coordinator of the University of Saskatchewan's MFA in Writing. My colleagues in the program.

Sage Hill Writing's participants, facilitators and staff. The Banff Centre.

Cathy Ostlere, Terry Jordan, Charlotte Gill, Barb Howard. Kim Suvan and Heidi Grogan. The late and infinitely kind Alistair MacLeod.

The publishers and editors of Canada's literary magazines and presses, for giving writers a home. My publishers, Al and Jackie Forrie, and the terrific team at Thistledown Press, a thousand times.

Sarah-Jane Newman, Gail Norton and Phyllis McCord, for seeing me through up-and-down times. My dogs, for daily walks. The coyotes out on the edge for inviting me to join them.

The art of Mary Pratt, Emily Carr, Auguste Rodin, Sonny Rollins, lessons in light and living.

Dave Margoshes, for all he does and is, and for always reading with the ear of his heart.

Mom and Dad, with love. My sons, Darl and Dailyn, for being. These stories are for you.

Photo by Shelley Banks

dee Hobsbawn-Smith grew up in a gypsy Air Force family and currently lives on the family land west of Saskatoon with her partner, the writer and poet Dave Margoshes. She has two sons.

Her award-winning poetry, essays, fiction and journalism have appeared in literary journals, books, newspapers, magazines, and anthologies in Canada, the USA, and elsewhere, in such diverse publications as *The Malahat Review*, *Gastronomica*, *Western Living*, and *Swerve*. Her debut collection of poetry, *Wildness Rushing In*, was published by Hagios Press in 2014. She recently completed her MFA in Writing at the University of Saskatchewan. Prior to that, she attended Sage Hill Writing five times. Her fifth book, *Foodshed: An Edible Alberta Alphabet*, which examined the issues and politics of small-scale sustainable agriculture, won Best Culinary Book at the 2013 High Plains Book Awards; Best (Canadian English-language) Food Literature Award in the 2013 Gourmand World Book Awards; and 3rd place in the 2014 Les Dames D'Escoffier MFK Fisher Book Award. She is at work on her first novel, *The Dryland Diaries*, and an essay collection, *Bread & Water*, which won 2nd place in the 2014 John V. Hicks Long Manuscript Award. *What Can't Be Undone* is her first collection of short stories.